Boarlander Beast Boar

Boarlander Beast Boar
ISBN-13: 978-1530970209
ISBN-10: 1530970202
Copyright © 2016, T. S. Joyce
First electronic publication: March 2016

T. S. Joyce
www.tsjoycewrites.wordpress.com

All Rights Are Reserved. No part of this book may be used or reproduced in any manner whatsoever without written permission, except in the case of brief quotations embodied in critical articles and reviews. The unauthorized reproduction or distribution of this copyrighted work is illegal. No part of this book may be scanned, uploaded or distributed via the Internet or any other means, electronic or print, without the author's permission.

NOTE FROM THE AUTHOR:
This book is a work of fiction. The names, characters, places, and incidents are products of the writer's imagination or have been used fictitiously and are not to be construed as real. Any resemblance to persons, living or dead, actual events, locale or organizations is entirely coincidental. The author does not have any control over and does not assume any responsibility for third-party websites or their content.

Published in the United States of America

First digital publication: March 2016
First print publication: April 2016

Boarlander Beast Boar

(Boarlander Bears, Book 4)

T. S. Joyce

ONE

Pain was a part of this life. Scars were, too. There was no soft, cushy existence for shifters, and especially not one for Mason Croy.

There was just this: ache, loss, longing, anger. Always anger.

Mason spat blood. He angled his neck, cracked it, and then stretched it to the other side to do the same again. "Call me pig one more time," he dared the three humans who'd lured him to the alley beside the post office.

The tall one held a bloody brick in his shaking hand, and his face was gore. It was that one who wouldn't shut up in the post office. He just couldn't let Mason pick up a package and leave in peace. Couldn't let him run one lousy errand without having to swallow all the slurs and names he and his backwoods buddies came up with. And one had decided to video tape him, right up to the point when he'd ripped the phone from his hands and chucked it against the wall, shattering it into a million satisfying pieces.

Red tinted the edges of his vision as one of the men circled around him. Mason wasn't stupid enough to get himself surrounded. Not when this one had brought a crow bar. Good. He hadn't had a good fight since the night at the fight barn. Wailing on Clinton was the only thing that had settled the fire inside him, and then he'd spent two damn months pretending he was okay. Pretending there wasn't some monstrous urge in him to destroy everything just to feel better. Pretending to be happy floating between Damon, the Gray Backs, and the Boarlanders. Fuck. Bash's sad face flashed across his mind, and he shook his head hard to dislodge the vision.

His boar raged to escape him, but he couldn't lose it like that. Not here. Crowbar lunged, swung hard, and Mason smiled in the instant he caught the cold metal and arched back his other arm. Finally.

The red in his vision turned black, and he was gone. He was driven only by instinct and pain. Something hit him hard in the back of the neck, but he wouldn't worry about the others.

Not now. With his knee on Crowbar's chest, he wailed on him.

Someone was yelling. "Mason!"

Fuck off. I'm busy.

"Mason!"

Mason lifted his fist. Crowbar wouldn't be crowing about what a freak he was anymore. He wouldn't spew to anyone else about how his people should be shoved in cages. He wouldn't talk anymore about shifter babies being put down or the government castrating the male monsters.

Mason was ripped backward so hard, his shoulder dislocated. Harrison's furious blazing blue eyes were there, but Mason was trying to look around him at Crowbar. The Boarlander alpha had Mason pinned against the brick wall with his forearm on his neck, but Mason wasn't done punishing that asshole yet.

"Stop it!" Harrison barked out, struggling to keep Mason from the anti-shifter humans. So much power in his voice, but his order washed right over his skin like a chilly wind. Silly alpha couldn't give a rogue an order. Mason belonged to no one. Belonged nowhere.

I'm nothing.

His attackers were running now, their weapons discarded in the muddy alley. In a puddle where the brick lay, shallow waves lapped at it, his blood spreading from the gray stone outward.

"I'm good," he gritted out.

"You aren't—"

"I am!" Mason shoved Harrison off and gave the alpha his back. Harrison didn't know it, but that was the biggest slight a boar could give. It was a sign of deep disrespect, but fuck it all, he shouldn't have pulled him off that anti-shifter scum. Mason slammed his fist against the brick.

"What's going on, man?"

Mason slid his bloody hands down the wall and squatted in the mud, gripped the back of his head to keep his skull from splitting apart. He couldn't Change here. Couldn't Change. Damon would be disappointed. Again.

What was wrong? He was being haunted. It had been ten years, but recently, Esmerelda had started showing up in his dreams, just as he remembered her, crying and sad. And right before he woke up in a cold sweat, she always said the same thing. *They're coming.*

Mason retched, then shrugged Harrison's hand off his back. He didn't want touch. Never had. Touch meant something different to boars. Touch was for mates, and he'd failed his a decade ago. And now she was back as an excruciating reminder that he hadn't been enough, and no matter how much he fought or Changed, it wouldn't help. He deserved this hollow feeling in his middle. He'd earned it.

"Mason," Harrison said, his tone softer this time. "What is it?"

Mason gritted his teeth and snapped his shoulder back into place, and the searing pain dulled the image of Esmerelda he had in his head. When he could see straight again, he dragged his gaze to Harrison. "I'm sorry," he said, his voice cracking. Chest heaving, Mason stood and stumbled toward a water spigot on the side of the building. He turned it on and cupped his hands under the cold stream. Right before he splashed it onto his face, he saw his reflection there in the clear water. He barely recognized himself under the full beard and empty eyes. Wincing, he brought his hands to his face and then reached for more of the spewing water to rinse again. Too bad the water could only wash away blood and not memories.

"Bash misses you," Harrison murmured from right beside him. "The girls, too. And me and Kirk. Hell, the trailer park isn't the same without you. It feels…empty."

Mason knew all about feeling empty. He'd just been really good at hiding that until recently.

"You moved out a month ago, and you haven't visited once," Harrison said. "And I hear things."

"What things?"

"How you are in the woods. Diem and Clara are worried, and the dragon doesn't say so, but I can see the worry in his eyes when I ask how you're doing. You aren't yourself."

Mason swiped the collar of his cotton shirt over his face for a quick dry and then stood and squared up to Harrison. "Yeah? And who am I?"

Harrison shook his head and shrugged. "I thought I knew. You were good with us, man. You were okay."

"Yeah," he rasped out, because for a while with the Boarlanders, he'd felt okay. He'd had purpose, and that was a big deal to a man like him. But logging season had ended, and now he was back to where he had been before, living in mountains where he didn't belong, where he floated on the outskirts like a ghost, never really a part of anything. "I'll come by. I'll see Bash and the girls, just...maybe give me some time." Because they couldn't see him like this. He was midway down one hellish spiral, and he hadn't hit rock bottom yet. He'd be damned if he dragged any of them down with him.

"All right, man," Harrison said, "I'll see you soon." He looked like Bash right now, his face all shadowed with sadness, and Mason ducked his gaze. He had to. He was carrying enough weight right now without feeling guilty over disappointing Harrison, too.

As Mason watched him walk out of the alley, he wished he was different. He wished his animal would settle. Wished he could be like Kirk and Bash, or hell, even Clinton. Wished he could choose a crew and allow himself to be a part of something bigger than himself. He wished he could be a Boarlander under Harrison, but his animal didn't attach to people like he should. He hadn't since Esmerelda.

Mason's pocket vibrated, and he gritted his teeth against the urge to pull his cell phone out and toss it into the puddle. He knew who it was before he even looked at the caller ID.

"Please tell me you didn't just send me to town to pick up a package that doesn't exist," Mason ground out as a greeting.

"There is a package, just not at the post

office," Damon said coolly.

"Spare me your riddles. What am I doing in Saratoga?"

"You need something I can't give you," the dragon-shifter said.

Mason snorted and leaned back against the gray brick of the alley wall. "You gave me a job, and friendship when I didn't deserve it. What else do I need?"

"Remember when you saw me struggling and decided it was time for me to breed a new female? You reminded me that I'm happiest when I'm raising offspring and caring for a woman, but that's not what you brought me when you paid for Clara to meet me. You weren't looking for a breeder. You found me a mate instead."

Mason narrowed his eyes suspiciously down the alleyway where Harrison had disappeared and pushed off the wall. "What did you do?"

"I have a new job for you."

"Well, if breeding a woman is what you have in mind for me, you and I both know I have a zero percent chance of succeeding at that."

"So they told you."

"No, so I know. I'm not having this

argument again. What job?"

"A driving job."

Mason inhaled deeply and made his way around a muddy bog and out onto the sidewalk of the main drag in Saratoga. "I'll be up there as soon as I can."

"No, Mason. It's not for me. I've hired a publicist to improve our public relations. We need it with the shifter rights vote approaching. You'll be her driver."

"Her." Mason pulled his sunglasses from where he'd hooked them on the back of his shirt collar before the fight. Huh. He couldn't believe they were still in one piece. Holding the phone between his ear and shoulder, he wiped a smear of red off the aviator lens and stepped out of the way of a stressed-out mother and two kids arguing over a plastic pony.

"Rebecca Edwards is waiting in front of that new Thai food restaurant for you to pick her up. Do try to be professional. You've let it slip lately." Damon had said it with an edge that made Mason shake his head and want to spit. Damon didn't even know how much Mason kept hidden. When he'd driven Damon around, he'd been about a million times more professional than he felt like being.

Mason jogged across the street toward his brand new Raptor. "Damon, I don't have the Town Car, and I'm not in my suit." With a glance down, he grimaced. His royal blue T-shirt was sporting a dark stain on the front, and warmth was dripping down from his hairline to his cheek. "I'm not exactly in professional mode right now. Sorry, old friend. You'll have to find someone else."

"There is no one else," Damon snapped. "Drive her or you're fired."

Mason locked his knees against any forward motion right beside his truck. Wow. Damon had never threatened to fire him before, and he'd been working for him for the past decade.

"Okay, I'll do it," he said softly.

"Good, and Mason?"

"Yeah?"

"Don't screw this up."

"Don't worry. I'll get the publicist to your mountains unharmed."

"That's not what I mean."

Mason frowned. "What do you mean then?"

"I mean, don't screw this up for you."

TWO

That couldn't be him. Beck squinted at the grainy photograph in the newspaper clipping. Emerson Kane had written about the shifters' battle with IESA. It included a black and white photograph of the Boarlanders, but Mason Croy's face was hard to make out. In the newspaper article, he was next to Kirk Slater, the gorilla shifter's arm thrown over Mason's shoulder. They were sitting on a porch step in front of a mobile home, so he definitely didn't resemble the towering behemoth jogging across the road toward a jacked-up black-on-black Ford Raptor.

The man was talking into a cell phone, his dark eyebrows lowered into a frown as he spoke too low for her to hear. He skidded to a stop and said a few more words, then pulled his cell phone away from his ear and stared at the screen. "Mother fucker." That part she did hear, as the words snapped to her on the wind.

That was him. Probably.

Except a helluva lot sexier than she'd imagined a pig shifter to be. Thick-soled work boots, long powerful legs, and a small, tapered waist drew her gaze up his muscular physique. His shoulders were massive, and his chest pressed deliciously against a thin blue V-neck T-shirt. He held a pair of sunglasses in one massive hand, and the phone looked like a baby toy in his other. That man was built like the Keller brothers of the Breck Crew, who were the only predator shifters she'd ever met.

Beck shouldered her purse and her two floral totes and pulled out the handles of her giant suitcases. Ready to meet the giant pig-man, she tugged the luggage and stabbed the concrete with her high heels in what she liked to think of as her power walk. "Mason?" she called.

His eyes snapped to hers, and she stumbled. The bright blue stunned her, but there was no way he was born with eyes that color. They were a wild, glowing blue that looked like flames. Her ankle went to ninety degrees in a deep sidewalk puddle, and she went down hard with a squawk. Ungracefully, she twisted in midair right before she landed with a splash hard enough to put her tailbone through her esophagus.

She squeezed her eyes closed and wished for thirty seconds in a time machine. When she eked her eyes open, the bearded behemoth was standing over her, zero humor in his eyes.

"Rebecca Anderson?"

"Mmm hmm," she said from under her pile of luggage. Her cheeks now felt like the surface of the sun. "People call me Beck."

Mason grunted as he ran his gaze down the length of her body. "What are you wearing?"

Beck pursed her lips and mentally flipped off the rain clouds that had dumped buckets of water on the town. "White dress slacks. They're my power pants."

Mason dropped his chin to his chest and arched his dark eyebrows up. "Your power pants are wet and see-through."

Shit! Squirming under the pile of her luggage only got her more tangled.

"Stop, stop, woman, you're making it worse," Mason muttered as he pulled one of the tote straps over her head and yanked her up into a sitting positon.

She was still struggling hard, though,

because she needed to cover up her cookie box. She hadn't worn her cutest panties today. Nudes went under white, so she'd adorned her pelvis with beige granny panties.

Mason snorted and then cracked a slight smile. That's when she got a really good look at his face. His beard had been taking up a lot of real estate, but from this close, she could make out the start of one impressive black eye and several gashes that were leaking slow streams of blood down his face. She flailed her arms, swatting at his paws. When he held his hands up in surrender, she asked, "What in the curse word happened to you?"

Mason blinked slowly and lifted those animated eyebrows of his. "Curse word?"

"Did you get in a fight?"

The blue in his eyes cooled, and he stood smoothly, taking her totes with him. Without a word, he picked up her suitcases like they weighed nothing more than dandelion fluff and strode toward his truck.

"Please tell me you weren't in some bar brawl with the protestors," she called, scrambling after him. One look down at her clothes, and she groaned. The puddle was a muddy one, and now she was smeared in dark water. She limped after Mason on a sore leg, gave up on looking professional, and pulled her sky-high heel off that foot so she wouldn't roll her ankle again. She whimpered as shooting pain zinged up into her knee with each step.

Mason threw her belongings—literally *threw* them—into the back of his truck. Her make-up was probably all broken now. She gasped out an offended sound. "Hey! Careful with the merchandise!"

Mason cast her a quick glance, then drew up short and frowned at her limp. Beck lifted her chin primly and tried to look unaffected when she took the next step.

"Humans," Mason muttered as he made his way to her in three giant-man strides.

"Humans what?" she barked out. He was being ridiculous and prejudiced, and even if he was the most striking, handsome, muscular, sexy... *Stop it.* Even so, he was being a pitstain.

Mason bent at the knees and picked her up, hands supporting her shoulders and behind her knees. She yelped and drew her purse over her nethers because, yep, she could see her beige grannies practically laughing at her. "Put me down!"

"I'm not watching you limp and whimper all the way to the passenger's side, lady." He lowered his voice and muttered darkly, "I have a dragon to skin."

Mason yanked open the door to his truck and dumped her unceremoniously inside.

"Ow!" She swatted his hand as it brushed her boob. "You are the worst driving service on the planet."

"Oh, so you've used every driving service on the planet?" He reached across her lap with the seatbelt, but she shoved him back when his beard brushed her cleavage.

"And furthermore," she said, good and furious now, "a pig shifter would have zero chance skinning a dragon."

"Boar shifter," he barked out, then slammed the door.

Shocked by his brash behavior, she stared at him as he marched around the front of the truck and pulled himself into the driver's seat.

"*And furthermore,*" he mimicked her, "today is my day off of driving, I have a splitting headache thanks to some asshole doing his damndest to put a brick through my skull, my best friend thinks he's a fuckin' matchmaker, but he missed the mark, and wide, proof the one person in the world I thought actually knew me doesn't actually know a thing about me! You aren't my type, lady."

She felt slapped. "W-what?"

"Don't worry about it," he muttered as he turned on the engine.

"You cuss a lot. And you're wrong about your friend setting you up. I'm here on a job, you jerk, and besides"—she clenched her left fist and lifted her ring finger, the one with her wedding ring—"you aren't my type either." Lie, and even she could hear it on her voice. Big, burly muscle man with sexy eyes and triceps flexing as he gripped the steering wheel. He was exactly her type, though she hadn't known until right now. So what if she was divorced and single? He needed to stop thinking the world revolved around him.

He glanced at her ring once, twice, then slammed on his brakes at a red light and clenched his jaw so hard a muscle jumped there. "Fantastic. Thanks, Damon."

Pissed off, she swung her purse around to throw it in the back seat, hitting him in the side of the face on purpose. Beck scrambled over the console clumsily as Mason complained, "Don't hit the driver."

"Driver, yeah. You know, you aren't the only one who's had a shit day," she muttered as she buckled her seatbelt in the back seat.

"That water puddle doesn't trump a brick smashed against my head."

"And whose fault was that? You can't be fighting, Mason! My job is to take care of the Boarlanders' public relations. To take care public relations for all the shifters in Damon's mountains, and minute one that I meet you, you're bleeding from a fight! Please tell me you weren't videotaped."

"I broke the phone."

Her mouth fell open, and she gasped out. "You can't break people's personal property!"

He made a clicking sound behind his teeth and shook his head. "You wouldn't understand, *human*. You're safe. Your people are safe. The government doesn't want to strip your rights, cage you, or sterilize your entire species."

Shaking her head, she huffed a humorless laugh and stared out the window at the town blurring by. He was so wrong. She had just as much worry about the vote as him, or she wouldn't have taken this job. It wasn't just his world that was burning. Hers was, too.

Beck cast a quick glance to the back of his neck. There was a massive amount of bruising and a deep gash. Shifters healed fast, so he'd taken a beating to have marks like that. "I think you should eat," she murmured.

Mason ignored her, the stubborn man.

"Fine, I'm hungry, and Damon assured me that you would take care of me."

"Chhh," he huffed out. "I can't take care of anyone." He'd said that last part low, as if he didn't care if she heard it. She knew that feeling.

"Drive-thru is fine."

The steering wheel creaked under his grip. He inhaled deeply, then asked, "What kind of food do you like?"

"Anything, you pick." She pulled her phone from her purse as he pulled a U-turn. He could think what he wanted about her being some kind of blind date for him, but she was actually in Saratoga to work. To help. To relieve Cora Keller of some of the pressure on her and the Breck Crew and to make a decent wage because she had bills to pay.

Beck called the printer back because she'd missed a call from them. She haggled prices to print calendars and settled on one that fit the budget Cora had given her. And after she hung up with them, she made yet another call to the head of Saratoga Parks and Rec because they'd been putting off her plans to include special events for shifters at the Lumberjack Wars, and she was not taking no for an answer.

More than once, she caught Mason glancing at her in the rearview mirror, but when he adjusted his dick, she figured it was just because the low V of her button-down shirt had slipped to the side and was soggily stuck, exposing most of her lacey bra and left teat. Great. With a dirty look for him, she covered herself back up and agreed to have a conference call with a couple of the higher ups at Parks and Rec to discuss the Lumberjack Wars. After Beck hung up, she opened her daily planner and added the one o'clock call for tomorrow's agenda. She was scribbling away at questions she wanted to ask in the notes section when Mason pulled into the drive-thru lane of a restaurant called Butters Beer Burgers and Shakes.

Mason leaned out the window at the intercom and said, "I'll have three number ones, no onions, a large vanilla shake, and one of those apple fried pies. No…two of those." Mason twisted around. "What do you want?"

"Oh, my gosh," Beck said, cracking a grin. "That was all for you? What a pig."

Mason narrowed his eyes to angry little slits. "Boar."

"I'll have a cobb salad with light Italian

dressing."

"God, are you one of those dainty fancy-pants women always counting your calories? Sipping on water, and then you're like, 'I'm stuffed.'" He shook his head in mock disappointment. "So boring."

Actually, she'd eaten an airport burrito a couple of hours ago and this food run was more for him than her, but he could think what he liked. "I'm boring? You ordered a vanilla shake. *Vanilla*." She shot him a challenging look but took the bait. "And I'll have a small strawberry shake."

Mason smirked and put in her order, then changed his to a strawberry shake, too. Competitive much? She hid a private smile as she logged onto Cora's shifter site from her phone. Beck was helping run it now that she was officially on the payroll.

Yelling carried on the wind. A chant. "Cage the shifters…stop the epidemic…" A group of twenty or so walked a tight circle in front of the hardware store a couple doors down. Beck's stomach curdled at the picket signs. One was of a bear with Xs for eyes and its leg in a giant trap. *Get them before they get us.*

Mason had his head carefully turned away, too, but his shoulders had gone rigid. Before she could change her mind, Beck reached forward and slid her hand over his tense arm. He was even harder than she'd imagined. Mason froze under her touch, didn't move a muscle for a moment, then leaned forward and out of her reach. "My people don't like touch," he said in a voice that was low and growly.

How sad. She couldn't even imagine a life without physical affection. Sure, her marriage had been like that, but she'd had Ryder, and he loved cuddling. Another deep ache cut through her stomach just thinking about him. Blinking hard, she hit her ex's speed dial and waited for the tenth time since she'd come to Saratoga to hear it ring and ring until his voicemail came on. "Hey, this is Robbie. If this is a booty call, leave a message. If this is Beck, fuck off." He'd always been so charming.

She plastered an empty smile to her voice, because screaming never worked with him. "Hey Robbie. I really wish you would change your voicemail. And maybe pick up your phone because I've called a bunch of times, and this isn't how it's supposed to work. I'm supposed to be able to talk to him still, just like I always let you talk to him when he is with me." She sighed deeply and prayed for patience. Robbie had been the worst decision she'd ever made. "Anyway, please call me back. I'm starting to worry. Okay, bye." She hung up the phone and relaxed into the back seat. Another flash of blue, and she caught Mason's eyes in the rearview again.

"Your husband?"

The last thing in the world she wanted to do was talk with Mason about Robbie and all the hurt and betrayal. She wasn't even sure if he was nice yet, or if he would judge her.

"You got a kid?" The SUV in front of them pulled forward, so Mason coasted up a car-length, too.

"So, I was thinking we should do more in the community," she said, typing away at her phone as she answered a question from the website about shifter hearing. "A bake sale or something, and give the profits to charity. I could call up the local news station and set up a couple of interviews—"

"I'm not doing interviews. How old is she?"

"I have a son, and why no interviews?"

He turned in his seat and locked eyes on her. "Because trust me when I say you don't want my people coming up into these mountains to retrieve me. It's best if we stay quiet about my whereabouts."

"Why would your people come after you?

Did you piss them off?"

He chuckled darkly. "You have no idea."

"Do you have kids?" She'd tried to research Mason, but his page on Bangaboarlander.com had been taken down a month ago. Even when it had been up, the picture of him was grainy at best, and all it had said was, *Good at fucking. Good at money. Great third best friend.* Wow, she couldn't believe she still had that memorized.

"No kids."

"Ahhh. A happy bachelor, no attachments. I get it."

"No, it's not like that. I want 'em. I just can't have 'em." A frown marred his face in the reflection of the rearview mirror. "I don't know why I just told you that."

"I'm sorry," she said, hunching at the angst in his voice. "Why can't you?" Good grief, what was wrong with her? That was so rude to ask a stranger.

Mason swallowed audibly. "I'm what my people call a barrow. The Barrow, actually. With real pigs, that would mean a castrated boar, but with boar shifters, it's just a title they give to males who are sterile." He shrugged one shoulder. "I don't talk about this stuff. Please don't let this conversation leave the truck."

"Of course. Was it...?" *Stop talking!* "Was it from an accident or something?"

"Nah. Bad genetics I guess."

"H-how did you find out?"

Mason pulled forward another car-length and rested his arm on the open window. "Because I failed to breed my mate, and then I failed with two sows after her. Three strikes, and you're a barrow."

Her voice dipped to a devastated whisper. "But why do they call you *The* Barrow?"

Mason gave her a glance over his shoulder that clenched her stomach. His eyes had darkened to a soft, chocolate brown, but were now full of ghosts. "Because I was supposed to be alpha over all my people. No more questions, Beck. I'm not a fan of revisiting my past."

And with that, Mason turned around, closed down, and hit the volume on the radio to drown out any further conversation. Beck rubbed her palm where she'd touched his warm arm. It was still tingling and hot for reasons she couldn't explain.

And as she looked down at her planner with the chaotic scribbles, she knew this wasn't just a job anymore. It was personal now. Mason had been through enough. He was a real person with deep, hidden aches. She couldn't do anything for his past, or his childless future, but she could fight for reprieve from the muck that had been raining down on him and the other shifters in Damon's mountains.

THREE

Outside the window, the buildings, streets, and protesters had given way to backroads and pine wilderness. Beck had been on the phone for a half hour working, but now she was caught up and the quiet was starting to get to her. Mason hadn't even eaten his food, so there was no crinkle of paper, no slurp of strawberry shake to fill the emptiness. He'd even turned down the radio, probably to let her talk on her cell easier.

"Are you always the strong silent type?" she asked.

"It's part of the job description. I'm paid to drive, not carry on conversation."

"I have a car of my own, you know. It's just in the shop. Cracked engine block and bad belt and a bunch of other things I'm pretty sure the mechanic just made up. Ripey's Auto Repair should be called Rip-Off's Auto Repair. My Explorer was just making a funny sound, so I took it in and, all the sudden, it wasn't safe to drive and has a billion things wrong with it. And he's charging me an astronomical amount. The mechanic says it'll be another two weeks before I get it back, so I had to take a shuttle service to Saratoga, but the driver said he wouldn't take me any farther than town because the mountains were haunted."

Mason kept his eyes on the road, didn't respond in any way. Determined to get back to the chatty Mason she'd talked to earlier, she gathered all her paperwork in the back seat into the right folders, then unbuckled and crawled ungracefully into the front seat. Beck pulled the belt over her lap and clicked it into place. "I thought I was sterile, too. I had a big cyst on my ovaries when I was sixteen and had to have surgery, so only one side works, and even before that I had a condition that makes my cycles patchy at best."

Mason tossed her a quick, bland look, so she said, "Right. Too much information."

A few more minutes of quiet drifted by, and she had to stifle the urge to open the window just to hear the wind.

"I'm divorced," she blurted out.

"Then why are you wearing that big ol' sparkler on your ring finger?" he asked as he pulled off onto a muddy dirt road.

"Because it's kind of new." She cleared her throat. "Actually, that's a lie. I've been divorced for over a year, and before that we were separated for two. And when we were married…well…he didn't come home much."

Mason pulled to a stop right before an old, creaky bridge, cut the engine, and got out. Oookaay. She startled when he appeared at her window and pulled open the door. Without a word, he yanked off her heels, unbuckled her, and scooped her up, then carried her to a wooden bench beside the bridge that overlooked a gently rolling river. "I'm hungry," he grunted.

"Oh, you don't like people eating in your new, fancy truck?"

"If I cared about that, I wouldn't have let you sit on my seats in your muddy clothes."

She looked down at her stained pants. Well, he had a point. Mason jogged back to the truck and returned with the bags of their food. His burgers and fries had to be cold by now, but when he sat down beside her and dug in, he didn't seem to mind. He gulped a bite and relaxed, one long leg stretched out on the soft earth. "You look young to be divorced."

Beck poured dressing over her salad and grimaced. "Divorces happen all the time now, don't you know? It doesn't care about age. I'm twenty-seven."

"How old is your boy?"

"Five," she said through a smile. She loved thinking about Ryder.

Mason's eyes were glued to the curve of her lips. Self-conscious under his gaze, she turned her attention back to stirring up her salad. "His daddy is no good, but Ryder is everything bright in my life. I had him when I was twenty-two. He wasn't planned, nor did I plan on anything long-term with Robbie, but we got married because that's what our parents said we were supposed to do."

"Ryder is a good name."

"You want to see a picture of him?"

Mason's lips turned up in a slight smile, the happy expression there and gone in an instant. "Sure."

Beck pulled her phone out of her back pocket and scrolled through her pictures to her recent favorite. In it, Ryder was squatted down by a patch of weeds, blowing dandelion seeds into the wind. She loved taking pictures of him. Mason stared at the screen, his expression unreadable.

"I thought I wouldn't be able to have a kid," she rambled. "And then I got Ryder, and I wanted ten more of him." She pursed her lips. "Me and Robbie tried. A part of me thought another baby would fix what was wrong with us, but that was just desperation in the end. He got a job traveling, working on pipelines right after we got married. He only came home on Saturday nights, and by Sunday morning he was off again." She shrugged as she remembered the pain of not being enough to keep him home. "It was mostly just me and Ryder, so being separated from Robbie didn't feel much different. And being divorced just feels like a failure, you know? I don't miss him because I never really had him, but taking the ring off means admitting defeat. I was in it one hundred percent, but he had…" She forked a tomato to death and sighed. "Sorry. I don't talk about this stuff either." She scrunched up her nose. "It's pretty embarrassing to admit that I gave half a decade to that man."

"He had what?" Mason asked, handing her back the phone.

"Robbie had other girls who kept his attention better. He said I was boring in the bedroom. He said I was boring at life."

"Oh, shit," Mason muttered, chucking his half-eaten burger back into the bag. He draped his arm over the bench on the other side of him and stared at the setting sun, shaking his head like he was disgusted. "I'm sorry I called you boring for ordering that salad earlier. That was fucked up of me. I didn't know."

"Think nothing of it, pork rind. I was unoffended. My skin got real tough. So tell me what I should know going into the Boarland Mobile Park."

He offered her a surprised glance. "Is that where I'm taking you?"

"Of course. That's going to be my temporary home."

Mason gave her power pants and her pink button-up blouse a once over. "You're going to live in a trailer?" The tone of disbelief in his voice was offensive and uncalled for.

"Yes, I am. But not ten-ten. Cora told me about its magic mojo, and I'm not looking for any of that. I'm going to set up shop in the other empty trailer."

"Trailers," he corrected. "There are two empties besides ten-ten now. I don't live there anymore, so my old house is up for grabs."

"Wait, what? I thought you were a Boarlander."

"No, Beck." He rocked his outstretched work boot from side to side and looked toward the river flowing under the old bridge. "I'm not an anything."

She studied his profile, from his short, medium-brown hair and his straight, proud nose to his thick beard. His chest rose with every breath, pushing his defined pecs against the fabric of his shirt, and his body was cast in the soft sunset glow. He was masculine and powerful, yes, but sitting here so close to him, he was more. He was rough around the edges, but underneath all that, he was a beautiful soul. She could tell these things. She had more instincts than he knew about because he assumed she was human.

"I know all about feeling invisible, Mason. Like you don't belong. But you aren't invisible. To me, you don't feel like *nothing*," she admitted softly.

Mason jerked his gaze to hers, and she could see his animal there in the flash of blue before it faded back to the natural dark color of his eyes. He didn't smile but, to her, he felt...relieved.

"I think maybe we should start over," she said. "We were short with each other earlier, but we will be living in close proximity in

Damon's mountains, and I want a good working relationship with you. I mean, not just you, but all the shifters. Including you." And now she was rambling, so she scrunched up her face and offered her hand. "I'm Beck."

Mason hesitated on touching her palm, but finally, he slipped his hand against hers for a shake and held it. "Mason."

Now the tingling sensation was back and, in an instant, it sparked too hot and she yanked her hand away. Mason stared at his palm with an intensity that said she wasn't the only one who'd felt it. He ran his thumb along his lifeline and murmured, "You don't feel like nothing either."

FOUR

You don't feel like nothing either? What the hell was he thinking? Mason needed to get away from this sexy siren, and quick. She was four years younger, and though that wasn't a deal breaker, she'd lived a completely different life than him. A hard life had made him feel ancient until Damon had saved him, and she was young and optimistic and beautiful. God, so beautiful.

He snuck another glance over to where she had set up a traveling office in the passenger's seat. Stacks of papers were everywhere—on her legs, on the floorboard, on the console. She had a purple pen stuck behind her ear, which kept her reddish-gold hair off her cheek, giving him a great view of her face. She was fine boned, and her skin fair and smooth. She had a smattering of freckles dusted across her nose and cheeks, and her eyes were the most alluring shade of seafoam green. Her eyebrows were a shade darker than her hair and delicately arched, and though she was petite, her soft tits were bouncing under her shirt with every bump he hit. He couldn't wait until they got to the extra shitty road in the Boarland Mobile Park.

Her lips were full and glossed in a deep shade of that pink shit Bash called "lip glitter." She smelled like vanilla body spray and some floral product she probably used in her hair and, fuck, he hadn't wanted a woman like this since he'd been a rutting breeder boar. Ten times already he'd imagined bucking into her against a tree, on the bench by the river, in the back seat, in his bed... God, his head was completely filled with her. He glared down at his massive boner throbbing against the seam of his jeans. Both heads, actually.

"Mason?"

"Hmm?"

"Did you hear me?"

"Uuuuh, yes. But just for fun, can you repeat whatever you just said?"

"I asked if you thought the boys would be okay with opening discussion boards on their bangaboarlander pages?"

"Beck, if you saw the kind of messages that come through there, you wouldn't ask that. All you would get is sex talk."

"Right." She clicked her pen and frowned down at a massive to-do list. She hesitated, her pen hovering over a bullet point. "No, you're right. That wouldn't be helpful." The long scratch of her marking it out filled the car.

He was actually flattered that she was asking his advice. He didn't know shit about public relations, but he liked how familiar she was with him when she talked. A wave of chagrin took him. She was a publicist and used to managing people. It was part of her job to be familiar with him.

Mason pulled under the Boarland Mobile Park sign and slowed on the nice, new, pot-hole-free white gravel road. Whoa. He leaned forward and squinted at the park. He hadn't been here in a month, and a lot had changed since then. The yards all boasted bright green sod and were freshly mowed, and someone had disposed of the pile of tractor parts and old car frames one of the old Boarlanders used to work on before Clinton had chased him off. The trailers had new roofs, fresh paint, and each yard had professional looking landscaping. All except Clinton's, where he had somehow burned the words *FUCK THE NEW RULES* across his front weed-riddled lawn. That was about right. He huffed a surprised chuckle. A part of him had missed Clinton, though he wouldn't ever admit that out loud. Clinton was a canker sore—always had been, always would be.

Even the chairs around the new bricked-in fire pit in front of 1010 at the end of the road were shiny, new, and in an array of neon colors.

"I expected something way different," Beck murmured, her eyes round as she gawked at the pristine park.

"Me too," he admitted. A slash of pain ached in his chest—he'd missed the last of the Boarlanders' transformation. He would miss everything. He needed to drop Beck off quick and get out of here before he started spiraling again. This wasn't his place. He worked for Damon and had his old room up in the dragon's cliff mansion.

Mason had no business aching for places that weren't home.

He puffed air out of his cheeks when Harrison came out of the first trailer on the right, followed by his tiger shifter mate, Audrey. Like a coward, Mason wanted to run.

Wanted to drop Beck off right here because emotions hurt. He'd felt almost normal here once, but now his animal was reacting to everything, and he couldn't be the one who dragged the Boarlanders through the mud with him. Not after they'd improved this much.

He let off a shaky, steadying breath, and beside him, Beck cast him a worried glance before she stunned him to stillness by placing her hand over his thigh. He came to a stop in front of the fire pit and fought the urge to pull away from her. This time, she didn't burn him with her fingertips. This time it was just warm. Comfortable. But still, he didn't deserve the touch. Couldn't handle it. He wasn't like the others. Slowly, he eased his leg away from her and did his best not to flinch at the ache in his middle from the hurt in her eyes.

"Look," he said in a hoarse voice. "You seem like the affectionate kind. Soft-hearted. But that isn't for me."

She opened her mouth to say something, but he held up his hand to cut her off. He couldn't hear it right now. Not when being back in the trailer park for the first time in all these weeks felt so overwhelming. Not when he was doing his best not to Change and show her what a monster he was. Not when it felt like his heart was beating out of his chest and everything was too bright.

Not when he still had to face the crew he'd abandoned.

* * * *

Beck sat there shocked as Mason fled his truck. She winced when he slammed the door. Her hand tingled again, so she rubbed it. What did that sensation even mean? She'd never felt it before, and now the man who was drawing her animal up couldn't wait to get away from her. No, she wasn't the human he thought she was. She just didn't have the kind of animal that smelled like fur, and she had fierce control over her eye color. A product of her upbringing. A product of hiding—from everyone.

Why was her animal screaming out possessively for a man who wasn't her match? His edges, as it was turning out, were too rough, too jagged. Painful, like serrated sheet metal, keeping her at a distance, and it had only been one day. Mason felt big, and terrifying, and he couldn't even bear her touch.

Stunned, Beck slid out of his truck. A giant of a man bolted from the woods and down the gravel road toward Mason. The man wore swim trunks and nothing else, had jet-black hair and green eyes full of an intensity she didn't understand. Maybe he was angry? She braced for impact as he hit Mason hard and hugged him tight, buried his face against Mason's neck. He was crying, murmuring something to Mason too low for her to hear. The boar shifter clapped him hard on the back and rocked them back and forth. Sebastian Kane was treating Mason like he hadn't seen him in years, and what was wrong here? Cora had assured her the Boarlanders were intact, but something had come along and split Mason off—that much was clear by the emotional reunion.

The other Boarlanders approached slower, as if giving Sebastian room to greet Mason as long as he wanted. She'd done her research, knew who they were from the pictures on the internet. Mason hadn't been easy to find, but the rest of them were out there for everyone to see, fully registered and open with who they were. Social media accounts, bangaboarlander pages, blogs, and newspaper articles. Emerson Kane was cupping the slight swell of her belly with one hand and wiping the corner of her eye with the other as she approached, all curly black hair and emotional gold-colored eyes.

And Harrison was there with his short chestnut hair and somber, dark blue eyes. His mate, Audrey, had her dark hair pulled high in a ponytail and wore a purple Moosey's Bait and Barbecue shirt over cut-off shorts. Kirk, the massive gorilla shifter who had made waves across the world a couple months ago when he battled Kong in animal form, stayed on the outskirts, eyes averted. He felt…angry, and Beck's fight or flight instincts kicked up. Warily, she pressed herself against the tailgate of Mason's truck and exposed her neck. His mate was human, but looked tough. Alison had short platinum-blond hair and tattoos on one arm that stretched from under her black tank top to her elbow. Her eyebrows were dark, and her pixie face held a similar frown that Kirk wore.

Sebastian shoved him back to arm's length and croaked out, "You're back now so I don't have to miss you no more. You're back now."

Mason looked gutted and shook his head. "No, man. I'm just delivering your new publicist."

Sebastian crossed his arms over his chest like a shield, and now he wouldn't meet Mason's gaze. He cleared his throat and cast her a quick glance, then back to the ground.

"Hi, publicist. I'm Bash." He gestured to Emerson, who was rubbing his back. "This is my mate and my cub. It ain't out of Emerson's belly yet, but it's still my cub."

"I'm Rebecca Anderson, but everyone calls me Beck." She stepped forward to shake his hand but stumbled to a stop when Kirk spoke up in a voice that was too low and too gravelly to be human. "You look great, man." There was a sarcastic edge. "I guess you've just been too happy with your awesome new life to come visit."

The truck bed sank and creaked loudly. A muscled-up titan stood in the back and slammed his dusty boot on the tailgate. He leaned forward, resting his forearms on his thigh. Clinton. "He don't look great." He twitched his predatory silver gaze to Mason. "You look like shit."

Mason ran his hand over his short hair and then shook his head. "It's nice to see you, too."

"Is it?" Clinton jumped out of the truck and landed hard on the gravel, kicking up dirt. He stalked Mason slowly. "Pretty shitty the way you left, don't you think?" He looked around to the others. "He don't write. He don't call." He shoved Mason's shoulder hard, but the boar shifter barely moved. "I guess spending a whole fuckin' logging season here didn't bond you to us. Not like we thought." Clinton lowered his voice to a shaking, angry murmur. "Not like *I* thought."

"Clinton," Harrison warned.

Mason ran his hand over his beard and said, "Nah, Harrison. It's fine."

Clinton began circling behind Mason slowly, and the air felt so heavy it was unbreathable.

"Don't," Audrey gritted out, but Clinton didn't hear, or didn't care.

A massive blond grizzly exploded from his skin and then paced ten yards off, eyes never leaving Mason. A challenge if Beck ever saw one, but she'd never been this close to a Changed grizzly shifter, and Mason stood no chance in a fight with Clinton.

Mason sighed, then pulled his sunglasses off and tossed them in the back of his truck.

Panicked, she pleaded, "Mason."

"Go on inside," he murmured in a dead voice.

"No, I don't think you should do this."

The Boarlanders had scattered, and now a smattering of pops pulled Beck's attention. A massive white tiger was stalking forward, head lowered, lips curled back over long canines and, holy shit, what was happening?

When she turned around to beg Mason to leave with her, to get in the truck and drive them away from here, he was peeling his shirt over his head. She was stunned to silence. Oh, she'd known he was fit from the way his shoulders filled his T-shirt, but she hadn't been prepared for him to look like this. Suntanned skin, rippling with muscle, defined abs that flexed with his movement, and two long, raised scars that stretched from his pelvis up his ribs and disappeared under his arm. His biceps bulged as he pulled his shirt right-side out, as though he had all the time in the world.

"Wait, wait, wait. I think we should go," she whispered, grabbing his hand without thinking.

He flinched away and gave her a warning look. His eyes were glowing blue, and power pulsed from his skin. "That trailer will do for you," he ground out, jerking his chin at the last trailer on the left. "Get on inside now. This don't concern you."

But he was wrong. It sure felt like it concerned her. Like anything that happened to him would hurt her, and she didn't want this. Didn't want him fighting against these apex predators. What chance did a little boar shifter stand against them?

"Mason, go easy on him," Harrison said.

Wait, what?

Harrison crossed his arms over his chest, his arms flexing with the motion. "Let him keep his innards."

Beck held out her hands in a beseeching gesture to the Boarlander alpha. "I guess I just don't understand why they need to bleed—"

Pop, pop, pop! A pulse of raw power blasted against her skin, and Beck hunched defensively. The dust had kicked up, but it didn't hide the enormous beast that rose up from the earth.

"Oh my God," she murmured, straightening slowly.

She'd imagined Mason's animal as a two-hundred-pound feral hog, but she'd been so wrong. The muscular hump between Mason's shoulder blades was taller than the bed of his jacked-up truck. Pitch black, coarse fur covered his body, and longer hair spiked up like a Mohawk down his back. Huge barrel chest, smaller back end, glossy black hooves, and when the dust settled enough and he looked over his shoulder at her, Beck's breath was sucked straight out of her lungs. He had long, curved, razor-sharp tusks and demon-bright blazing eyes full of undiluted rage.

She'd been so wrong. He absolutely stood a chance against these predator shifters because Mason Croy was a beast. Emerson grabbed her hand and yanked her toward the trailer, and then Alison was there, hand on her back, urging her forward faster.

"They're gonna fight," Beck murmured, stunned.

"Yep, that's what they do."

"But they're friends," Beck argued. "Friends don't fight."

Alison and Emerson shared a loaded look, and they all hunched under the deafening roar of a grizzly.

"Shit," Alison muttered. "Run now. They aren't careful brawlers."

In horror, Beck realized what she meant when a loud clash of animals locked in battle swung their way. Panicked, Beck bolted beside the girls and took the porch stairs two at a time. She froze in the doorway as Audrey's white tiger leapt onto the boar. Bash's black-furred grizzly burst from him, and he charged with a speed that was dizzying. "Three against one," she murmured. "That's not right." Not fair. She should Change and help, but what difference could she make in a battle like this? Her animal wasn't like theirs.

"Not three against one," Emerson rushed out. "Bash and Audrey are trying to keep them from killing each other. Clinton has been on a tear since Mason left. He has no control. And Mason feels…" She shook her head. "He doesn't feel right."

Harrison was in the fight now, and Kirk had Changed into a massive silverback, pacing the outskirts on long, powerful arms and legs, his eyes blazing gold.

Beck couldn't decipher who was winning. The white gravel road was speckled with blood, and the roaring of the bears rattled the park. They were all so fast, so lethal, their movements blurred, she only got flashes of the battle. Audrey with her claws sunk deep into Clinton's back. Bash swiping a massive claw at Mason's front hooves just before he lunged his tusks into Clinton's exposed belly. Bear slaps echoed through the trailer park and then, in an instant, it was done.

Harrison shrank into his human form and yelled, "Change back. Now!"

The result was instantaneous as Clinton and Bash shrank back into their human skin with pained grunts. Audrey, too, but Mason refused, lifted his tusks higher, and glared down Harrison.

"Please," the alpha said breathlessly, putting pressure on his bleeding hip.

Mason shrank back but landed hard on his knees.

"Fuck!" Clinton yelled, gripping the underside of his right arm. Red streamed through his fingers as he glared at Mason, then struggled to his feet. "You did this. You made this place Hell, just like I knew it always would be. It wasn't the girls who screwed us. It was you! You're the reason Bash can't smile anymore. You're the reason Harrison's so quiet. You're the reason none of us can look at your damned trailer without feeling empty, why the girls won't say your name, why Kirk can't stop his Changes." He jammed his crimson-soaked finger at Mason. "You're the reason my chest hurts. I didn't break the Boarlanders. *You* did." Clinton spat red, and with fury in his silver eyes, he strode off toward the trailer across the street with the burns in the yard.

Mason disappeared behind his truck, and when he reappeared, Harrison was following closely behind. Mason wore his jeans, but his shirt was still MIA. He yanked Beck's belongings out of the back and strode toward the porch she stood on.

"Clinton's having a hard time," Harrison said.

"Yeah, and you think I meant for any of this to happen?" Mason barked out, rounding on the alpha. He looked from one face to the other as the Boarlanders gathered around in a loose half-circle, tugging on clothes, averting their gazes, completely silent.

"You think I'm hurting you on purpose? Really? My animal is so fucked up right now I have no control. All I want to do is fight and wash away everything that's going on in my head, and I'm stuck *feeling* all this shit I don't know how to deal with. My time here made that harder. It made me too soft. I wasn't trying to hurt you!" Mason shook his head and looked like he was about to retch. He lowered his voice. "I was trying to protect you."

Slowly, Mason set her luggage at the bottom of the stairs and dragged a hollow gaze to Beck. "I can't be your driver. I'm sorry."

With that, he spun on his heel and strode back to his truck, then peeled out of Boarland Mobile Park, leaving a trail of dust in his wake. Leaving a trail of friends in his wake. Leaving Beck with a strange hole in her middle that felt as if it would never be filled again.

He didn't know it, nor would he ever, but her animal had chosen him. And for the millionth time in her life, she hated being a shifter. Hated not having control of her body, of her heart.

Because her animal worked on pure instinct and didn't understand that Mason Croy, the untouchable beast boar, was the worst decision she could make.

FIVE

Mason paced his room. Down to the minutest detail, it looked the same as it had before Damon's enemy, Marcus, had torched the mansion. Damon was like that, though—thorough, detail oriented, a perfectionist.

He should call Beck. He should apologize and explain, but no. That would require talking about Esmerelda, and he wasn't there yet. He wouldn't be able to say what he wanted without Changing and ruining everything. Again.

She shouldn't have seen his boar that soon. Beck was a classy human not used to the fighting. She wouldn't understand that he and Clinton had needed to bleed each other. That it was instinct, and that it fixed more than it hurt.

A soft rumble rattled his chest. She

shouldn't have been there. And why the fuck had Cora and Damon thought an unmated human belonged in Boarlander territory anyway? It couldn't be to tempt the shit out of him because he didn't even live there. Didn't visit there.

The heavy double doors to his room swung open, and Damon glided in uninvited. He had a tendency to do that since he wasn't used to being told "no." The dragon simply did what he wanted and, apparently, right now, what he wanted was to piss off Mason.

"What happened yesterday?"

"Nothing. I did as you said, got Beck to your mountains safely. I even fed her."

Damon pinched the thighs of his charcoal gray dress pants and lifted them an inch before he sat on Mason's bed. His eyes were lightened to the silver of his dragon, and his pupils dilated in that eerie way that reminded Mason of a snake. Apparently Mason's animal had the dragon in Damon riled up, which was one hell of a dangerous game to play.

"Clara has told me something unsettling."

"That the new chef sucks? Because he does, and he's an asshole."

"You've never had a single complaint about my staff before, nor have you had a problem getting along with anyone. Clara says you have a ghost problem."

Mason stopped his pacing and leveled Damon with a calculating look. Damon's mate was a clairvoyant. Or maybe a psychic or a seer, but she could definitely see ghosts. She'd seen all of Damon's phantoms the second she'd set foot in his mansion a couple years ago.

"I don't know what you mean."

"Young, dark hair, dark eyes, beautiful. She follows you around but only late at night when you're getting ready for bed and are about to sleep. Clara says she sees her clear as day, and while my mate doesn't know your whole story, I do. And I would be willing to bet Esmerelda is part of the reason you are struggling now. Tell me I'm wrong."

Mason swallowed hard and whispered, "She was beautiful."

"She also died ten years ago."

"Yeah, and how long before you moved on from your first mate? Huh? How long until you moved on from Feyadine?"

"It was different for me."

"Why?"

"It just was."

"Tell me why you were allowed to mourn

your mate like you wanted, and I'm not!"

"Because I had all the time in the world to mourn her. Centuries if I wanted them. You have one short life, Mason. Ten years is enough. Maybe it was too much." Damon gripped the edge of the mattress and leaned forward, eyes softening to a medium gray. "You aren't supposed to live your whole life alone. Esmerelda wouldn't have wanted that. If she's here now, it's because you made her spirit restless. You conjured her by hanging on too damn tight. Let. Her. Go." Damon stood to leave, but when he reached the door, he turned. "I want you out of this house."

"Are you firing me?"

"No, old friend. I'm setting you free. You will be Beck's driver. You will move into your old trailer at the Boarland Mobile Park, and I'll pay you the same salary I do now. You're using this house as a crutch. This job as a crutch. Me...as a crutch."

"That's not true. I owe you."

"You owe me nothing. Surely, you understand you weren't ever just my employee. I didn't take you from your asshole people because I pitied you. I took you because you needed a friend, and I needed that, too."

"It's not as simple as just moving back there, Damon."

"Do you know what happens to a tree that never succeeds in putting down roots?"

It dies. Was Mason dying inside? Hell, it sure felt like it. He'd figured out how to survive, but living was something that had always stayed just out of reach. He'd been closest to it when he'd spent a season logging with the Boarlanders.

But...

Mason had left for a reason. He'd been dreaming of Esmerelda, and he didn't want Harrison and his crew to feel the effects of his downward spiral. The Boarlander alpha already had enough on his plate with Clinton and trying to bring his crew out of a deep, dark hole. They had their own problems to overcome, new mates, and intricate new relationships that only worked if one of the crew wasn't dragging them all to Hell.

Mason stared out his window at the wilderness, shaking his head over and over in denial of what Damon was doing. He was pushing him to take his baggage and his damned ghost to a trailer park of misfits on the cusp of becoming great. He was a poisoned arrow Damon was launching at the heart of a beast, and damn it all, Mason didn't want to hurt them.

Beck was going to *see* him. They all would. They would see all the ugliness he'd been hiding because he was incapable of keeping it in the shadows anymore. For years he'd been stoic, easy-going, dependable Mason. That was the character he'd played, but that side of him was unreachable now. He didn't have control over anything anymore.

For reasons he couldn't understand, he revolted against the thought of Beck watching him break, but maybe Damon was right. Maybe it was time to throw away the crutches and make an honest effort for something more than the half-life he'd settled for.

Mason scrubbed his hands down his face as he looked around his room—the one that had never felt like home. "When do you want me out?"

"Now." Damon's lips thinned into a straight, somber line. "I want you to start living now."

SIX

"Hello?"

Beck stopped fiddling with the sheets on the bed of 1010. "Robbie?"

"Obviously. You're the one calling me."

"Yeah, sorry." God it was still so weird to talk to him. They'd cared for each other once. A long time ago. And now co-parenting would force them to always be in each other's lives. She had to keep things cordial. "I've called a few times—"

"A few dozen times."

She cleared her throat and counted to three so she wouldn't remind him in a scream that he was supposed to let her talk to her son. "I've been calling because I wanted to see how it was going and talk to Ryder. I miss him a lot." So much more than she was admitting out loud, but right now, just the idea of getting to finally talk to him and hear his squeaky little voice had her heart ripping apart.

"It's my month. I get one a year, so the least you can do is let me enjoy it without you breathing down my neck."

"Yes, I totally understand that, and I'm glad you are stepping up—"

"Stepping up?" he said in that deep, familiar timbre of his. "I've always provided for him, have I not?"

"Well...no. You've only made one child support payment, and it was thirteen dollars and a Snappy Freeze Yogurt coupon. Anyway, as I was saying, I'm really glad you asked for the month and are putting an effort into spending time with him. That's what I want. For you to have a relationship with our son because he loves you and deserves to have you in his life. But you know how when I have him and you decide to call, if I'm able, I always let you talk to Ryder? I guess I thought it would be more like that. Where I wasn't just cut out of his life for the entire time you have him."

"Yeah, well, you can't talk to him right now. I'm working."

"Wait, working? You said you were going to take time off. Where are you?"

"None of your damned business, Beck. I'm

working a few more days at this job, and then I'll go pick him up from my parents. He probably hasn't even noticed I'm gone. This is how we've always done it."

Yeah, with him being gone. "Why did you ask for him if you aren't willing to spend time with him, Robbie? I don't understand. Is it to hurt me?"

"Goddammit woman, not everything is about you."

"I'm not trying to make it seem like that. I'm really not. I just don't understand why we went through all of that mediation if you aren't even taking time off to be with him. And don't tell me it's to spend more time with your parents. I love them. They are like a second set of parents to me, and I let Ryder see them whenever they ask. I just don't understand why I'm spending an entire month away from our son when you aren't with him." Rage was bringing her blood to a slow boil, and she needed to end this call, quick. "No, you know, it's fine. I'm sure he's having a great summer with your parents."

"He is. He's having a great fuckin' time. I just talked to him two days ago, and they were taking him to the zoo."

Two days ago. *Two days ago*? It was

supposed to be Robbie taking his son to the zoo! Not "checking in" with him every few days via phone. He'd done that shit Ryder's entire life, and her disappointment that he hadn't changed was infinite.

"Hey," Robbie murmured in a softer tone. That was his go-to voice when he wanted favors. Cuss at her, but then go smooth and ask for some inconvenience of her. "Since I have you on the phone, I wanted to talk to you about something."

"What is it?" she ground out, debating hanging up now and blaming a bad connection.

"I'm gonna be in Saratoga on Wednesday. I know you're stayin' close to there, so I was wondering if you'd like to meet up. To talk. About Ryder."

Well, that was new. Robbie usually did his best not to see her at all. She'd even been dropping Ryder off with Robbie's parents when he wanted him on the occasional day or weekend, just so her ex could avoid her. He wasn't the best, or most mature, co-parenter. "What about Ryder? Why can't we just talk on the phone about it?"

"Because it's important, and I have paperwork."

"Robbie, I swear to God if you're taking me to court for primary custody—"

"No, it ain't like that. I'm good with a month in the summer."

She huffed a soft noise and shook her head. She wished she could reach through the phone and strangle him. A month? He would probably spend five days with his son out of that month. She'd made a huge mistake with her ex, and Ryder was always the one who got hurt by her bad decision. "I just don't understand why we can't talk about it now."

"You got better shit to do than talk about your kid, Beck? You're the one always actin' so high and mighty, perfect parent. Are you just having so much fun partying while he's away, you can't give up one night to focus on him?"

This time she counted to five so she wouldn't say a bunch of words to Robbie McFartFace that started with "Fs" and ended with "uck yous." He'd always been the partier, not her.

"I'm not up here partying. I'm working. You know, for money? That's the green stuff I need to raise *our* child, and if you call him 'your kid' one more time, I'm going to explode. He's ours. Ours, ours, ours!" Because her dumb ass hadn't insisted he wear a condom when he was a whiny twenty-year-old who didn't like using them. She loved Ryder. Loved him more than air, but damn it all, she wished she'd had him with a man who cared about people other than himself. "I can't raise him on hopes and dreams, Robbie! And you don't pay child support. You give me no help, so yeah, when you have him, I have to go lady-balls to the wall working my ass off so we can be okay. So I can afford our apartment, so I can pay our bills, so I can save up for the puppy he's been begging for the last six months, so I can feed him and take him on vacation someday." And here came the waterworks because Robbie always did this. He always made her feel completely alone.

"I want to talk about his animal!" Robbie yelled into the phone.

Beck gasped and clamped her hand over her mouth to keep her sobs inside. He'd never wanted to talk about Ryder's shifter side before. He'd always avoided it like the plague and cut her off anytime she mentioned it.

"You want to know why I'm not with *your kid*? I left for work because the day I was supposed to take him to a park, he got mad at me and Changed. And what am I supposed to do with him when he's like that? Huh, Beck?

You want me to stick him in a little animal cage and take him around with me? Introduce him to the other little normal kids? Explain to everyone why I'm carrying around a fuckin' pet to the kiddie park?"

God, she hated how he talked about Ryder's shifter. "How long was he Changed?"

"All fuckin' day!"

"Well, did you make him upset?"

Robbie got real quiet, and that was answer enough. He knew better than to lie. He knew she could tell if he did. Poor Ryder. Beck would bet her bones Robbie had been shaming him for the tiny animal in his middle, and Ryder had escaped the rejection the only way he knew how. Twin tears streamed down her face, and for the first time since she'd met Robbie, she admitted to herself that she hated him. But all the hate in the world didn't change the fact she had to co-parent with this person. No matter her feelings, Ryder needed a relationship with his father.

"Fine. Where do you want to meet?"

Robbie sighed a relieved sound and said, "I don't know the area. You pick."

She didn't really know it either besides what she'd researched. "Okay. There's a bar the locals like to hang out at. Sammy's."

"Boring Beck meeting at a bar?" he asked in a baiting murmur.

"Don't call me that. I'm not boring. I'm not yours anymore, Robbie. You don't get to put me down like that."

"Pissy, pissy. Meet at Sammy's then. Nine o'clock is good with me. I'll be staying the night at a bed and breakfast outside of town."

"I have a big photoshoot scheduled for that day, so keep your cell phone on in case I'm running late."

"Well, don't run late!"

Arguing with him was pointless. Everything was on Robbie's schedule. Her life had orbited around his convenience, and he would never change, so utterly defeated she said, "Okay. I'll be there."

Robbie ended the call, and she set her cell phone down gingerly. And then she allowed herself to do something she had desperately been trying to avoid. She cried. And not the soft kind either, but the curled on the bed, arms wrapped around her stomach kind. She missed Ryder, and she worried about the way Robbie was treating him. She was here in a strange place with a shifter culture she didn't know. How did she feel this lonely around people of her own kind? She'd thought it would be different if she was around other shifters. But now all she felt was this immense pressure to help them, which put a barrier between them. She was the publicist, the employee, other, and they were a close-knit crew whose friend-cards were all filled up.

And Mason...

Her animal was pining for him, which made everything harder.

A light hand touched her back, and she jerked and gasped. And then as if her thoughts had conjured him, Mason was there, right beside her on the bed, his eyes dark and sad. "Are you okay?" he asked.

Are you okay? How long had it been since anyone asked her that? "How long have you been here?"

Mason looked uncomfortable and wouldn't meet her eyes. "I heard your phone conversation, both sides. I didn't mean to. I knocked, but you didn't answer, so I came in and waited for you to hang up."

"I didn't hear you knock, and is that how a trailer park works? People just barge in whether you want them to or not?"

"Pretty much." Mason relaxed against the headboard and clasped his hands over his stomach, crossed his ankles. His boots were hanging off the bed, he was that tall. "What are you doing in ten-ten? I thought you didn't want any of the magic on you." Was that a spark of humor in his eyes?

"Yeah, well, have you seen the empty trailer? Clinton has been using it as a workout room slash woodshop slash karate studio. The place has been destroyed by Kung Fu Clinton. There was zero room for me to work there, much less live."

Mason's voice softened. "Why didn't you move into my trailer?"

Beck rolled over on her side to face him and curled her knees up to her chest. She wiped her damp cheeks on the sleeve of her pale pink hoodie and sniffed. "It just didn't feel right. That's your place. I went inside, but it still looks like you never left."

With a slight frown, Mason asked, "What do you mean?"

"I mean, there are even rinsed dishes still left in the sink, the bed is still unmade, and someone's been feeding your mouse. It even smells like you. And Bash looked gutted when I was considering it. I don't think they've given up on you coming back. Ten-ten is fine if…"

"If what?"

"If there is a chance that you'll move back

here someday."

Mason inhaled deeply and stared at the window unit AC on the opposite wall. "Your ex sounds like a dick."

Beck snorted, and the stretch of her smile felt good. "I like dicks. In my head I call Robbie 'McFartFace.'"

Mason chuckled a deep, resonating, sexy sound, and she watched his smile spread up to reach his eyes. God, she bet he was beautiful under that thick beard.

"Can I tell you something?" she asked softly.

With a single nod of his chin, he tightened his arms over his chest and murmured, "Sure."

"I was kind of scared I would never see you again. And I know that sounds stupid because we barely know each other, but you were the first one here to talk to me, and I feel weird around the others, butting in and ordering them about. Plus, eating lunch with you by the river the other day was kind of amazing. It was nice to just talk easy with someone. Talking with you was…comfortable."

Mason was quiet for a long time before he said, "I like that you say what you mean. No lies or half-truths. You just lay it out there."

"Most people don't like that about me."

"I think it's brave. I couldn't do that."

She laughed and shook her head. "You have me pegged wrong. I'm the biggest coward in the world." She hadn't even told Robbie she was a shifter until Ryder Changed for the first time, and now she was hiding from Mason, too. Typical Beck. So scared of what people thought about her that she couldn't own what, and who, she was. No, the shifters of Damon's mountains were brave. Mason was brave. She would spend her whole life hiding from the world.

"Your car will be ready in a week, and they knocked down the price by half."

Confused by the turn in conversation, she propped up on her elbow and asked, "What do you mean?"

"I mean, they really should be called Rip-Off's Auto Repair because they were squeezing you big-time. That asshole mechanic would've dragged it on for another month, too."

She sat up, stunned that someone had done something nice for her. Something that actually helped her. "You took care of it?"

"Yeah, I tracked down the shop yesterday. I didn't know you lived in Douglas."

"You're surprised I'm small town?"

"Hell, yeah. From your fancy power pants,

I pegged you as a big city girl, come down from your high rise to free the shifters."

"Ha! No, but I did come down from my second floor apartment a few hours away to try and help. This is my first experience ever in a trailer park."

"Exciting, isn't it?"

"Very. Did you know there are two mice in here that prefer jalapeño potato chips to the healthy mouse food I've been trying to feed them? I think they are addicted, and it makes me like them more because jalapeño potato chips are friggin' delicious."

Mason's grin grew bigger. "I did know about Nards and Nipple's love of junk food."

"And did you also know that Clinton might be a bona fide psychopath? I caught him ripping a rosebush out of my landscaping in the middle of the night, and he tried to convince me it was all a dream. And then he flipped me off and went back to his trailer. And this morning when I woke up to have my coffee on the porch, he climbed onto the roof of his trailer and pissed right off the front into his yard. And he smiled at me as he did it."

Mason laughed and rested a hand behind his head, relaxing bit by bit beside her. "I definitely know he's a psychopath. He'll grow on you, though."

"And did you know Bash really, really misses you? He's asked me if you've called about a dozen times. I tried to explain to him that you aren't my driver anymore."

The smile faded from Mason's lips. "Yeah, I knew that part, too. I'm moving back into my old trailer." He heaved a sigh and rolled his head toward her, leveled her with a somber look. "I give it a week, and they'll wish I would've stayed gone."

Beck dipped her voice to a whisper. "You're not as broken as you think, Beast Boar."

The corner of Mason's mouth ticked up and, slowly, he reached for her, pushed her hair back off her cheek with the barest brush of his fingertip—his first voluntary touch. "You're wrong."

SEVEN

The trailer park was a ghost town right now, not exactly the return Mason had imagined, but this was better. It would be easier for everyone if he slid back in quietly. He'd had a hard time ripping himself away from Beck after she'd been so open with him. After he'd heard the conversation with her ex. After talking to her until she drifted off to sleep, right there in the middle of the afternoon, as though she felt safe with him. After he'd tested himself, touching her cheek and reveling in the warm, comforting sensation that drew up his dick.

He couldn't push too hard with her, though. If her quiet sobbing after she had gotten off the phone with her ex was anything to go by, Beck had been wounded badly. All Mason had been able to think about all afternoon was covering her, fucking her until she screamed his name and forgot about that douchebag who talked to her like she was nothing. Asshole didn't even realize what he'd lost. God, Mason hated people like him. Robbie. He wanted to rip his throat through his mouth-hole for calling Beck "boring" again.

Beck was the most interesting woman Mason had met since Esmerelda.

Letting off a steadying breath to cool his blood, Mason pulled a moving box from the bed of his truck and took it inside his trailer. The second he stepped through the doorway, he froze. Such a strange sensation washed over him, prickling his skin. His room at Damon's house hadn't ever felt like home, but this place…this dilapidated, thirty-five-year-old singlewide came pretty damn close.

He set down the box and ran his fingers over the neck of his old guitar in the corner, and then along the back of the couch to reacquaint himself with the place. It smelled like wood polish, floor cleaner, and soap. Someone had been in here to keep the dust at bay. Bash, he would guess, and an accidental smile took Mason's face at the vision of that big clumsy brute in here with a dust rag, humming off-key to himself.

Mason made his way to the bedroom, and sure enough, Beck had been right. His covers were still unmade, just as he'd left them. A vision of Beck on her hands and knees, back arched and wet sex ready for him flashed across his mind, and there it was again—that instant boner. Geez, he felt like he was a rutting breeder again since she'd stumbled into his life in that fucking sexy, muddy, see-through outfit of hers. Was that was this was? Maybe he was rutting, encouraged by his broken boar, or from how damn fuckable Beck was. He had to be careful with that one. She wasn't some sow in heat. She was human. Fragile. He would have to open her up slowly. Fuck. *Stop thinking about her like that. She isn't yours.*

But he wanted her to be. And she had Ryder, so maybe she wouldn't be as disappointed in the fact that he couldn't give her a child. She already had one. Mason winced at the pain of that thought. He'd missed her being pregnant. Missed that entire part of her life, and why did that seem like such a huge thing? If he went after her, he would never see her belly swell with child. Would never press his hand against the movement there. Would never be there for her when she gave birth. She would never bear a child with a tiny piglet just waiting to present itself in that first year of life. Maybe he was biased, but boar shifter babies were the cutest.

Stop it! He couldn't lose his mind over things that would never come to fruition. Beck wouldn't have his child. No one would. That wasn't the life that had been meant for him. At least she had Ryder. Good strong name, and Beck was a good mom for gifting it to him. Something inside him said that McFartFace hadn't come up with anything so good.

"They're coming."

Mason hunched and spun, but no one was there. It had been Esmerelda's voice, just a whisper over the drone of the AC unit. Chills blasted up his skin as he narrowed his eyes and searched the kitchen behind him. Shit. She really had followed him here, just like he'd feared. He would have to call Clara and ask if she knew a way to get rid of her. Or maybe he would pay Jason of the Gray Backs a visit. He'd somehow banished the ghost of a dead ex-mate a couple years ago. Or maybe Beaston, who saw so much more than everyone else, would have some advice for him. Mason had to do something because Esmerelda had only visited his dreams until now, and she'd never been powerful enough to speak to him in broad daylight.

His inner boar roared to Change. To fight…something.

If it was the last thing he did, Mason had to protect the Boarlanders from whatever was happening to him. He had to protect Beck from his past.

Outside, trucks rumbled through the trailer park, siphoning his attention away from the empty kitchen. *Here we go.*

Mason made his way out of his trailer and locked his arms against the porch railing. He watched the parade of cars filter into the park. The dumbfounded looks and slow smiles on his crews' faces as they drove past made him think that maybe Damon had been right sending him back. If Mason ignored the skittering fear that he would hurt the people he cared about, this feeling of homecoming was actually nice. And about now, he would take any balm for his soul, no matter how temporary.

Beck opened the door of 1010, and her eyes immediately locked onto him. With a boner-inducing smile, she lifted her hand and waved. Mason's heart beat against his chest. If that woman even knew how his beast was laying claim to her, she would run away as fast as those long, sexy legs could carry her.

He nodded a greeting and twitched his head, inviting her over. She should see this—the good, bad, and ugly. She should see the celebration at him moving back in, sure, but she should also see the shit the Boarlanders would give him for leaving in the first place.

She'd said she felt weird around the crew, and that had to change. Mason needed her to fit in here for selfish reasons, and he didn't give a single fuck what that said about him.

"Mason!" Bash yelled at the top of his lungs. He waved his arms all around like Mason could possibly miss the titan hanging out the window of Harrison's eye-scorching red pickup.

Mason waved back and jogged down the stairs to the new sod on his front lawn.

The trucks skidded to a stop, kicking up dust, and the Boarlanders piled out of them like an ant colony hunting a cherry flavored sucker. Mason couldn't help his laugh when Bash picked him off the ground and slapped him on the back hard enough to beat the air from his lungs.

"You C-Team again?" Bash asked, his voice heartbreakingly hopeful. "Tell me you're movin' back, Mace!"

"I'm back, Bash Bear. I ain't leavin' again."

Bash let off a long relieved sob, and his shoulders shook as he hugged him harder.

"Aw, come on, ya big crybaby," Kirk said, peeling Bash off Mason. "Let him breathe."

Mason stumbled to his feet and winced as the gorilla shifter gripped his shoulder hard enough to grind his bones. "Leave again, and I'll kill you." Kirk had said it through an easy smile, but his voice was completely serious and utterly believable.

Harrison pulled him in for a manly, painful hug, but the girls were much gentler, holding on longer, wiping the corners of their eyes after releasing him. And then Beck was there, eyes full of emotion, and that's how Mason knew she was a good one. She was affected by a dynamic she knew little about. She was rooting for him already. Rooting for all of them.

Before he could change his mind, he wrapped his arm around her shoulder and kissed her forehead, then released her and grinned at her baffled smile. She looked drunk as a skunk, and all he had to do was hug her. God that felt good—having a woman like Beck react to a simple touch from a man like him.

He had to get better. Had to, because she wouldn't settle for a broken man. She deserved better. Everything faded away as her full lips curved up in that smile he was falling in love with. She was the prize. If he worked hard enough, and long enough, maybe she would open up her heart to him. He couldn't offer her much, but he would treat her a helluva lot better than her ex if she gave him half a chance. He had to earn that chance first, though.

"You know how obnoxious this one is?" Bash asked, rubbing his giant hand over Beck's hair, mussing her gold-red curls. "She gave us one of them itittyaries—"

"Itineraries," Emerson corrected.

"And then Beck said we have to take sexy lumberjack pictures for some calendar and told us to manscape. Manscape!" Bash doubled over with a single bellowing laugh. "I had to Internet-search what that even meant. Emerson gots to shave my chest tomorrow morning."

"Oh, my God," Harrison groaned, scrubbing his hand down his entire face.

"I ain't doin' it!" Clinton said from the outskirts of the group. "I don't want to be part of some project to get the ladies all masturbating while they're looking at my sexy body. No thank you."

"Well, you have to," Kirk said lightly. "Damon and Cora said we need to do what Beck says, so if you want that paycheck to pay for all the pointless shit you buy, you can take a picture."

"Well," Beck cut in, her cheeks blazing a shade of red Mason had never seen on a human before, "the idea is to garner positive attention. We'll give all the proceeds to a charity you choose. I'll build it up real big online because the ladies in this country can be a powerful ally. They are outspoken about what they like, and they can give us a huge push in votes for reinstating shifter rights. So them—touching themselves if that's what they want to do—is good because that means they would see you as men and not animals."

"Ew." Clinton crossed his arms and looked grumpy. "When you say 'touching themselves,' it sounds pervy. Just say masturbate. That's what it is."

Beck's eyes went dead, like she wouldn't be baited.

Clinton got a predatory smile. "Say it, and I'll take one picture. Come on, publicist. Have a little fun. Say masturbate."

Beck was the color of a cherry and gritted her teeth. With an impressive eye roll, she gritted out, "Masturbate. And now you'll be January."

"What's January?" Clinton asked suspiciously.

"You'll be up against your fancy new truck, half-naked, wearing your hard hat, ripping your chainsaw in front of your crotch. And the photographer I hired will be taking your picture at the crack of dawn so it looks colder. You'll be up first."

Clinton scowled but didn't argue, and that was some progress right there.

"We should celebrate," Audrey said, her grin infectious.

"Celebrating nudie pictures?" Bash asked, looking from one face to the next. "That's weird, but okay!"

"No, Bash Bear," Audrey said through a giggle. "Celebrating Mason's return."

"Return of the pig!" Bash crowed, throwing his hands up in the air.

"Boar," Mason corrected for the billionth time. Bash's filter was broken.

Harrison draped his arm over Audrey's shoulders and said, "There's a new home cookin' restaurant that just opened ten minutes from Moosey's we could try. That Jam's Chicken House place. I think it's BYOB."

"Bring your own boobs," Bash said excitedly. "I call Emerson!"

"Good God, you moron," Clinton muttered. "It's bring your own beer."

"Fried chicken and mashed potatoes," Beck said tiredly. "The perfect pre-photoshoot food."

Everyone scattered quickly, on the hunt for six-packs to load up, but Beck's smile was sad as she watched the chaos.

"What's wrong?" Mason asked. "You know they'll still have hard-bodies even if they ate all the fried chicken in that place. Shifter metabolisms and all."

"Yeah, I know." She squeezed his hand gently. "I'm glad you're back and that your crew is so happy. Have fun tonight."

Beck made to head back to 1010, but he grabbed her fingertips just before she slid her hand out of his. "What do you mean? You're comin' too, woman."

"Oh, but this is crew business, and I'm not..." She swallowed and looked around the park. "I have work to do, anyway."

Mason arched his eyebrows pointedly.

"I don't want to be a burden—"

Mason leaned down and pressed his lips to hers to quiet her protests. Beck froze under him, her lips in a stiff line, but little by little, she melted against his side, and her lips turned soft. He cupped the back of her neck, reveling in her taste. Squaring up to her, he pulled her tight to his chest and pushed his tongue gently past her lips. And then he smiled against her mouth because she let off the fucking cutest little needy sound in her throat. He'd pulled that noise from her. Him.

Gripping the back of her hair, he brushed his tongue against hers one last time and eased back. Resting his forehead on hers, he kept his eyes closed just to savor the moment. Oooh, Beck Anderson felt huge to him. Bigger than he'd realized until he'd kissed her. "You're part of the craziness here now, Beck. You're coming to dinner with us. Go on, hop in my truck, and I'll get us some beers."

"Okay," she murmured. She was gripping his wrists hard, like she wanted him to stay, and damn, something about this little vixen was calling to his boar.

He let her go, gave her his most charming smile, and sauntered off toward his trailer. If he'd stayed locked up with her another minute, he was gonna say something dumb about how she already felt like his and scare her off.

And the thought of Beck leaving now was unimaginable.

EIGHT

Mason draped his arm around the back of Beck's seat and leaned onto two legs of his rustic ladder-back chair. The Boarlanders had eaten dinner on a long table against the far wall of Jam's Chicken House. It was one of those old-fashioned restaurants with dark wood walls, exposed rafters above, vintage street signs hung everywhere, mismatched tables, and checkered table clothes. There were only a few options for dinner, and all the sides and biscuits were served family-style.

Everyone was cutting up, ribbing each other, laughing louder than anyone else in the restaurant, and for the first five minutes, she'd debated reminding them they had a public image to uphold, but she'd decided against it. Let them laugh. Let them have a good time. If nothing else, the people in this restaurant could see the Boarlanders genuinely enjoyed being together. That's if they ignored Clinton's scowl and the soft snarls that occurred when someone got too close to one of the predator shifter's food. She supposed big, burly loggers required a lot of calories.

Beck had barely heard a word throughout dinner. She was too enamored with watching the curve of Mason's lips as he talked through that slight smile that dumped a whole heap of mushy feelings into her middle. What she wouldn't give to see him under that beard.

She touched her lips with her fingertips and remembered the kiss he'd surprised her with. It was one of those life-altering moments. It was a kiss she would compare every other one to from here on. No man had ever kissed her like that. Like he wasn't trying to get into her pants, but was just content to taste her and touch her instead. She'd always wished desperately for Robbie to be affectionate with her. Showing love wasn't his style, though, or maybe he hadn't ever really loved her. She'd assumed Mason's aversion to touch meant he was the same, but it was plain and clear that he was nothing like Robbie. She could tell by the way his lips had softened against hers, by the way he'd held her tight, as if he didn't want to let her go. She could tell by the way he had filled her plate without even asking before his own while he talked with Bash. She could tell by the way his thumb rubbed soothing circles on her back every once in a while just to let her know he was there, right beside her.

As if he could hear her thoughts, he ran his fingertips against her bare arm, trailing fire with his touch.

When she went to grab a sip of her beer, Clinton was frowning at her from across the table, his head canted as if he'd never seen her before. His eyes narrowed to little slits. When Audrey said something funny down the table, Mason laughed beside her, but Clinton lowered his voice and said, "Your eyes sure look strange in this lighting."

Shit! Beck dropped her gaze immediately. She'd lost herself in Mason's affection and hadn't realized he was drawing her animal to the surface. She was usually much better at concealing herself than this.

"What did you say your name was again?" Clinton asked low.

Beck ignored him and rested her elbow on the table, cupped her neck, and avoided his curious gaze.

"Oh, I remember now. Rebecca Anderson."

"What are you doing?" Mason asked in a hard tone.

Clinton was apparently too busy tapping away on his cell phone to answer.

A soft rumble sounded from Mason. He turned to her, drew her closer, and whispered right up against her ear, "Don't let him get to you." His bottom lip brushed her sensitive earlobe, and she sighed as heat pooled between her legs. And now there would be no hiding her eyes because her animal was desperate to drink in more of her mate.

Beck closed her eyes and clutched onto his shirt. Mason slipped his hand over her fist, squeezed her gently, and left his cheek against hers. His beard was rough against her soft skin. "I've never kissed a man with a beard before," she whispered.

His chest was heaving curiously under her hand, and he pressed her palm against his drumming heart, content to stay near her. Beck was shaking now, her muscles twitching to be even closer to him, and somehow, in the busy restaurant, the chaos fell away, and it was just her and Mason.

Eyes tightly closed, she whispered, "You make me feel…" What could she say that wouldn't send him scattered to the wind? Happy, normal, hopeful, like she could be good at love, like she didn't have to be alone, like she could share her whole self with someone for the first time in her life...

"I make you feel what?"

She could do this—*be brave*. She didn't want to hide from Mason like she had with Robbie. Mason was like her. He wouldn't judge her or look at her like she was disgusting. He wouldn't be disappointed. Slowly, she eased back, determined to let him see her eyes. They would be the color of liquid gold right now, an admission that she wasn't what she'd pretended to be. That she wasn't human. With a deep inhalation, she fluttered her eyes open.

Mason froze, and the relaxed expression on his face faltered with confusion. He cupped her cheek and ran his thumb under her eye, brushing her lashes delicately. Her pupils would have shrunk to pinpoints by now, and the strange color undeniable.

"Beck," Mason murmured.

She heaved breath as fear blanketed her. This wasn't like her. Not like her at all. She was at a table of predator shifters, and she was small and fine-boned, fragile compared to the goliaths talking around them. "Don't tell," she pleaded pathetically.

He searched her eyes, his own gaze lightened to a stormy blue now, as if her animal was calling to his boar. He swallowed hard, his Adam's apple dipping low before he said, "Okay. I won't."

And just as she moved to escape to the bathroom, he pulled her in close and kissed her.

"Bangaboarlander dot com strikes again!" Bash crowed from a few seats down the table, and Beck ended the kiss with a frantic smack of her lips.

Mason pulled her close, hiding her face from the others as he dished out, "Bash, she didn't find me on your stupid website."

Focus, focus, focus.

"Besides, we aren't exactly banging." Mason's tone sparked with humor. "She's just beggin' me to do the photoshoot tomorrow. Without words. Thinkin' about my lumberjack body got her all revved up, and I was just helpin' her—ow!" he said, wincing away from Beck's swat. He broke out in a laugh with the others.

Beck giggled and shook her head, feeling more in control of herself. But when she looked at Clinton, he wore an empty smile and murmured, "Well, you ain't registered."

Mason kicked him hard under the table. Clinton grabbed his shin and launched into a muttered string of F-words.

"Can I have your autograph?" an eight-year-old boy asked from over Clinton's shoulder.

The sandy-haired, grumpy behemoth formed his lips like he was about to say, 'No,' but Beck spoke up for him. "He would love to!" And then she glared him down. He was *not* going to make a public scene this close to the shifter rights vote.

"Fine," he gritted out. With a put-upon sigh, Clinton snatched the pen and paper from the boy and said, "You better not sell this on the Internet until it appreciates to a million dollars. This is the one and only time I'll be signing one of these." He scribbled his name across the paper and then spent some time doodling a cartoon of a bear who was…doodling. There was a smiley-faced poop glob and happy looking flies involved and everything. Lovely.

"Cool," the boy drawled out, staring wide-eyed at the crude treasure in his hands. "You're really good at drawing, mister!"

Clinton crossed his arms, practically

gloating under the compliment. He tossed Mason a competitive smile. "I'm good at everything."

"Okay then," Mason muttered as the server made her way to the table. She held up the check, and Mason gave her a two-fingered wave. "I got this."

"Oh, I can get my own," Beck murmured.

Bash loudly slurped the last of his water and piped up, "Don't worry, Beck. We can't break his bank. Mason is a boar shifter."

With a frown, she asked, "What do you mean?"

"Boar people only think about money and piglets. Mason is rich like one of them pirates with the buried treasures in the—"

"Bash!" Mason barked out. "That's good, man."

Bash was quiet for about two and a half seconds before he leaned forward and whisper-screamed, "He has lots of money."

Emerson and Audrey snickered, but Mason didn't seem amused. He sighed an irritated sound, pulled his wallet from his back pocket, and handed the waitress his card.

"They're coming," a woman murmured behind Beck.

"What?" she asked, turning around. Behind

her, no one was there. There was only an empty table, but when she looked at Mason again, he was staring at her with a look akin to horror in his now blazing blue eyes.

"Did you hear her?" he asked, an edge of panic in his voice.

"Who?" She checked behind her again, but clearly she'd lost her mind because, really, not a soul was there.

Mason shook his head hard and muttered, "No one. Forget it."

Mason signed the receipt in a hurry and then stood so fast his chair went up on its back two legs and toppled over.

"Are you okay?" she asked.

"I'm fine." His tone had gone feral. With a quick glance at Beck, he said, "I need some air." And with that, he turned and left the restaurant. Left her staring after him wondering what had just happened.

A cool breeze blasted against her neck and lifted all the fine hairs on her body.

Beck searched the empty space one last time as her instincts screamed that something wasn't right.

They're coming.

Who the hell was they?

NINE

The silence in the cab of Mason's truck was so thick it was choking. His profile was rigid as he gripped the steering wheel tighter, and his jaw clenched as he turned onto the road that would lead to the trailer park.

He was a powerful, masculine man with his ripped torso pressing against his white T-shirt, his suntanned arms bulging against the sleeves, so what on earth had him reacting like this? He'd closed down so fast, so hard.

"Do you want to talk about it?" she murmured.

Mason shook his head and pulled a baseball cap from the backseat, then pulled it low over his eyes. He wasn't hiding anything from her, though. Her senses were tuned to him already.

"I'm not rich, you know. It's not like I'm

just slumming it out here in the trailer park. I like living here. Like living simply. I don't need a lot."

"I'm not judging you."

Mason blasted under the Boarland Mobile Park sign, a trail of dust billowing behind them. "Bash was right."

"About what?"

"About what is important to my people. Boar people aren't like bears, or gorillas, or anyone else. Money trumps all, but wealth isn't only measured in the size of your bank account. Wealth is measured in the number of offspring you can successfully have and provide for. I don't have the offspring, but my instinct to stock away money is still there. I just don't have anyone to spend it on. I bought this truck, sure, but what else do I need? What else could I want? I had a big fancy job once, a long time ago. It hurt me, and it hurt…"

"Your first mate?"

"I don't want to talk about her."

"How long ago?"

"Beck," he gritted out, casting her a hard warning glance.

"Okay, I understand. You're not ready. It's hard to talk about my ex, too."

"Your ex, Beck. Ex. You're a shifter in

hiding, but still, you've never once called him your mate to me. I lost my mate. My *mate*. And when she passed, it ripped my guts out. Ripped my heart from my chest. Ripped my life away, my future. I was ruined by age twenty-two. That's what love does. Do you believe in ghosts?"

"Y-yes," she forced out, clenching her hands against the urge to shove open the door and flee. She couldn't be a shifter with all these heightened senses and not believe in the veil.

"When you lose love—actual love—your life gets filled with them. You see your mate on everyone's face you pass in the street. You can't stop thinking about moments you shared. Can't stop thinking about what-ifs. Can't stop blaming yourself."

Anger lashed at her heart that he was comparing his loss to hers. They weren't the same, but he didn't know how deeply she'd been cut. "And now she's haunting you."

Mason clacked his teeth together and pulled to a stop in front of 1010, and before the wheels had even locked up, she shoved open the door and scrambled out. Clutching her purse to her stomach to keep her pain from leaking from her body, she strode toward the porch. And when she heard him slam his door and follow behind, she jogged to escape him.

She reached for the door handle, but Mason was there in a blur, hand on the barrier. "You're angry."

"Damn straight, I'm angry," she said, shoving off him to get some breathing room. "You think you're the only one with real estate in 'actual love'? You think you're the only one who lost it? I loved Robbie. *Loved* him. Lucky you, your mate loved you back, but mine didn't feel the same about me. So no, I can't call him my mate because I wasn't that to him. I wasn't enough! And don't you fucking talk to me about ghosts, Mason. I can see my ghost. I share a child with him, have to talk to him, see him, watch him move on with some woman younger and prettier than me. I have to feel the slap of his rejection constantly, and I will have to bear it my whole life. He couldn't stand to touch me! Couldn't stand to fuck me unless it was from behind and he wasn't looking at my face, and I knew what he was doing. He was buried in me, thinking about the women he kept on the road. He spent more on them every holiday than on me. I could see our bank accounts, knew what was happening, but my animal was in it. I was trapped. I was mated.

He was not. I'm sorry you lost your mate. I really am. My heart bleeds for what you've been through. But I think that somewhere along the way, you became so buried in your own pain that you can't see the good things that are sitting right in front of you."

"Like what?"

"Like me!" Tears streamed from her eyes, and angrily, she wiped them with the back of her hand. "You lost your mate, and I'm sorry for it. Not because I pity you, but because I care about you. I don't want you to hurt because I know what the ache of loss can do to a person. What it can do to your animal. You lost a mate, and I know it's not the same to you, but I lost one, too. And now I'll lose another."

"What do you mean?"

Miserably, she ducked her gaze. In a shaking voice, she whispered, "You know what I mean."

Mason approached slow, and she countered back until her hips hit the porch railing. "Tell me."

Her face crumbling, she swallowed a sob and said, "I picked you the first time I saw you. I picked another man who can't pick me back."

And as he took another step toward her,

she gave into the pulsing power of her animal. She would be damned if another man ever trapped her.

****

Mason held his hands out soothingly, palms up, because Beck smelled different. He was hurting her, just like he knew he would. She smelled of anger and sadness and something more. Something inhuman. Beck hunched inward and imploded in an instant. Her clothes dropped to the floorboards and a massive white owl blasted toward him. She used his shoulder to leap from, her long, curved talons slicing through his flesh before she beat her powerful wings and caught air. She lifted easily, gracefully, glided to the tree line. He'd never seen anything more beautiful. She was larger than any wild snowy owl by five times, at least, and her wingspan was massive. Flowing downy feathers covered her outstretched legs, and her talons looked like daggers. And just before she disappeared into the night, she let off a surprisingly guttural and fierce call.

Holy. Shit.

Shifters like Beck were thought to be extinct. Most of the animal shifters were, and though some flight shifters still existed, like falcons and ravens, snowy owls hadn't been seen or heard from in decades.

I picked you the first time I saw you.

Mason ran his hands over his baseball cap, took it off, and chucked it at the trailer. He hadn't been paying attention. He'd been in the muck, trying to tread water and keep his shit together. He'd been concerned with taking it slow because, until dinner tonight, he'd thought Beck was human. They were different. Humans ran on slower timelines, so he'd been fine with push-and-pull in an attempt to get her to stick around. He wanted to try and become a good man for her eventually, but her animal had already picked him. She'd picked him? At his worst?

Him—a haunted beast boar with no roots.

Him—a sterile widower unable to let go of his past.

Him—a man who had no shot in hell at keeping a woman like her happy.

It made no sense. Yeah, their physical chemistry was off the charts in molten lava territory. His head was consumed with thinking about covering her, but Beck had seen through all his grit, and her animal had somehow latched onto him despite his one-way ticket to rock-bottom.

His timeline had just shrunk to nothing. He didn't have years or even months to figure out what was wrong with him. He needed immediate improvement so he wouldn't cause the hurt he'd seen in Beck's eyes just now.

She'd been right. He'd been so focused on his own decade-old loss that he had assumed her divorce was less-than. God, he was an idiot. He'd witnessed her heartbreak after her phone call with Robbie, and he was really preaching to her about "actual love"?

He hooked his hands on his hips and stared into the woods where she'd disappeared into the dark canopy. The deep talon marks on his shoulder burned like fire, but he deserved the pain, as well as the scars they would leave. Beck was a fierce beasty, and though a part of him surged with pride, another piece of him was ashamed he'd drawn her animal out of her like that. He'd been throwing his words at her, telling her in his own fucked up way, "You don't understand," and he'd been so wrong. She was a feeler. Her heart was full of deep emotion and empathy, and he'd mistreated that quality about her instead of coveting it.

Warmth trickling down his shoulder and soaking his T-shirt. Mason jogged down the stairs to his truck, and then he blasted down the road toward Grayland Mobile Park. He had to fix this.

Mason had to start fixing himself before he lost her because she wasn't alone in this bond. Beck—his beautiful, fierce, feathered Beck—had been so wrong.

He *had* chosen her back.

And it was up to him to do this better than her first mate because she deserved the effort.

She deserved everything.

TEN

Mason pulled open the door to Jason and Georgia's screened-in porch. It creaked loudly, but just in case Jason hadn't heard it, he knocked for good measure.

Georgia answered, clad in flannel pajamas, her wild curly hair piled on top of her head. A warm smile took her lips immediately. "You look like shit."

Mason snorted. "Thanks."

"No really. I mean, your beard looks rugged and manly and all, but you look like you haven't slept in a week."

"Is Jason around?"

Her delicate eyebrows lowered, and she pursed her lips. "Mason, I've heard about you in the woods. I don't really want Jason Changing with you until you have more control."

Mason nodded and ran his hand through his hair. He couldn't be mad at Georgia. He really had been out of control, picking fights with anyone who even looked at him. "I'm not here to ask him to Change with me. I just need some advice."

Georgia's gaze tipped to the gashes on his shoulder, and with a slow, worried blink, she nodded and called out, "Jason. Mason's here to see you."

Jason appeared out of the back bedroom a minute later, wearing jeans, no shirt, and toweling off his hair like he'd just gotten out of the shower. "Hey, man. You okay?"

"Yeah. Listen, can I talk to you?"

Surprise slashed through Jason's dark eyes, but the towering bear shifter recovered quickly enough. "Sure. I'll be right out."

A minute later, Jason was closing the door gently behind him and carrying a cold six-pack. "Come on," he said lightly, pushing past Mason in his bare feet, his back still covered in droplets of shower water.

Jason didn't say a word as he led him through the Gray Back woods behind the pristine trailer park, nor did he push conversation as they walked side by side, right through the porch light of Beaston's trailer.

The wild-eyed bear shifter was sitting on his porch, the door open behind him, and the soft glow from inside casting his face in shadow. All except those unnerving, glowing green eyes, which stayed on something behind Mason. Chills blasted up his neck, and Mason rubbed the skin there just to put warmth back into it.

"She ain't here for what you think," Beaston said low.

Mason looked behind him, but there was nothing there but the chilly feeling of wrongness. "What do you mean?"

Beaston lifted a shoulder. "You tell me." He stood gracefully and crossed his arms over his chest, cocked his head. "I would come with you to the treehouse, but this is as far as I can get away from my raven boy."

Mason smiled tiredly. He wished he had a baby to raise, but he was happy for Beaston. He was a good dad. Protective. "It's okay, man."

"Boar," Beaston said as he and Jason moved off.

"Yeah?"

"She didn't do it to hurt you." Beaston shook his head sadly. "Some people just feel too much. Hurt too much." Beaston climbed up the stairs and murmured, "She's saying sorry."

He closed the door behind him with a quiet click, and Mason clenched his shirt, right over his stomach where pain threatened to double him over. Beaston saw too much. Way too much. Mason had never told anyone that Esmerelda had taken her own life. He hadn't even told Damon how she'd died.

"I didn't know," Jason said softly.

Mason tried to smile but failed. "No one does."

Jason smelled of heavy sadness now so, unable to stand it, Mason strode past him toward the treehouse Beaston had built a couple logging seasons ago. He scaled the ladder and settled onto the porch, high up in the canopy, and dangled his legs off the edge. And when Jason had popped the tops on a couple beers and they'd each taken a healthy swig, Mason asked, "How did you get rid of your ghost?"

"I didn't get rid of her. She had to decide to leave on her own. I don't know, man. I blamed myself for her haunting me, but really, that was just Tessa's personality to spend her afterlife pissin' me off. She got louder and stronger when I first met Georgia, and then something changed." Jason set his beer down with a hollow clunk, then cracked his knuckles. "The harder I fell for Georgia, the weaker Tessa got, until one day, she could barely talk to me. I was letting her go, sure, but in a way, I think she saw me moving on, and she was letting me go, too. I used to hate her. Tessa was my maker, my mate, but I wasn't her only mate."

"Oh, shit," Mason muttered.

"Yeah, she died when she was with her other man, and she was mad I didn't come to save her when things went south. Hell, I was mad at myself for a long time about that, too, but it wasn't my fault. It wasn't her fault. It was a rival crew who didn't care about killin' off the women. The point—I used to hate her when she was alive. I hated her at her funeral because she'd bonded us, broken me young, and then she'd left me. Left me for another, left me on this earth mourning a woman who treated me like shit, but I couldn't get her out of my head. I hated her for haunting me. For making me think Creed would have to put me down when I went crazy enough. But in the end, she saved me."

"How?"

"She had something to say that was worth listening to, Mason. Georgia and Harrison?

They're here because Tessa warned me Georgia was in danger from those poachers. You remember that. You were there. Damon's mountains went to battle, and it was Tessa who told me to Change Georgia to save her. To save me. I didn't hate her in the end because, it turns out, she was there for a reason."

Mason sighed and dangled his beer bottle over the side of the porch. "So you think Esmerelda is here for a reason. Because she has something she needs to say?"

"Does she have words?"

"Only two, but they're getting stronger. Tonight at dinner, Beck heard her."

"Beck? The publicist?" Jason's lips twisted in a slow smile. "You bangin' her?"

Mason looked away to hide a smile. "None of your damned business."

"So, no. Zero pecker strokes for the sad pig."

"We aren't there yet, jackass. I want to be. She's all I think about…"

"But Esmerelda?"

"But lots of things."

"Like what?"

Mason gritted his teeth. He hated exposing himself to anyone, but he'd come here for Jason's help, and he owed it to Beck to try.

"Like she has a kid. And an ex who hurt her badly. Who still hurts her. And I'm…" Mason took a long swig of his beer, stalling. "I'm not good for anyone right now, and I don't want to add my baggage to her already complicated life."

"Who wants an uncomplicated life? I'm serious, man. Who wants a boring existence?" Jason arched his dark eyebrows. "The complications? The little blips and hiccups and heartaches? Those are what add texture to a life and make it good. They make people strong, make them able to appreciate happiness. And someday, when you get your head out of your ass, you'll be grateful for where you've been. Hell, you'll even be grateful for the time you had with Esmerelda because, in her own way, she's prepared you for this."

"For what?"

"For seeing the life you want and leaving the grit behind so you can go and get it. What does Esmerelda say, Mason?"

He stared at Jason, utterly shocked by how insightful the Gray Back jokester was being. "She says, 'they're coming.'"

"They're coming," Jason repeated softly. "Beck and her kid."

Mason swallowed over and over, afraid his voice would crack when he spoke. "You think Esmerelda's telling me it's okay to move on?" God, what was this feeling coursing through his veins? Hope? He almost didn't recognize it. Hope had eluded him for a long damn time.

Jason gripped his shoulder and shook him slowly. "Yeah, man. She's letting you go. It's time to let her go, too."

ELEVEN

Beck sniffed and wiped the last of the dampness from her cheeks as she shoved her legs into her jeans. The air had cooled up here in the mountains of Wyoming, chilling the floor boards of 1010's front porch, making the soles of her feet tingle.

"I saw you," Clinton said.

Beck gasped and pulled her pants up as fast as she could. Mortification blasted heat through her body in a wave before it landed in her cheeks. "Great, you pervert. You saw me."

Clinton frowned. In the dim porch lighting, he stood leaned against the rail near the bottom stair like he'd been there all night. It was eerie how quiet he'd been. She wasn't snuck up on easily, but her shame at what she'd done to Mason had her head spinning like a top, distracting her from the dangers of the Boarlander woods.

"I didn't mean I saw you naked. I meant I saw your animal. I knew you were a flight shifter. Just didn't know what kind. A snowy owl." His natural hate-filled scowl had morphed into an expression that looked almost impressed. Clinton cocked his head and narrowed his eyes, which had lightened to silver. "You're sad. Why?"

"I don't want to talk about it." With Clinton or with anyone else. She would need to leave this place. Run. Flee back to her old life where she felt steady. Here, she dared to want things that would never come to fruition for a person like her.

Clinton looked off into the dark woods. "You know, I had a girl once who was sad. She thought bottling up hurt meant she was strong, but it didn't." Clinton dragged his inhuman eyes back to her. "Silence will hurt Mason, and it'll hurt you, too."

Warily, she approached the side railing and looked down on the normally furious bear shifter. "Why do you care? I thought you didn't like me."

Clinton snorted. "Don't matter who I like, Beck. It matters who Mason likes. He's a jackass." He twitched his head behind him toward the trailer park. "They all are." Shrugging one shoulder up to his ear, he lowered his voice and murmured, "But they're *my* jackasses. Mason's known that quiet sadness before. It brought a strong man to his knees, and he hasn't learned to stand yet. I can see him trying with you, though. Don't break him before he gets there." And without another word, Clinton ripped the one remaining rosebush out of her landscaping, threw it in the middle of the yard, roots up in the air, then sauntered to his trailer next door and disappeared inside.

As his door banged closed behind him, Beck released the breath she'd been holding. Up until a minute ago, Clinton had terrified her, but maybe Mason had been right when he'd said Clinton would grow on her.

Break him? She didn't have the power to break Mason Croy. What Clinton didn't know is that she'd marked him. She'd claimed him because her animal required scars. She was a monster. And now the only one at risk of breaking here…was her.

What the hell had she been thinking? Everything had become so clear as she'd soared high above Damon's mountains, lost in her swirling thoughts of the man she loved.

What had possessed her to fall for a huge, dangerous boar shifter? She and Mason came from completely different worlds, obviously, and her decision to claim Mason didn't just affect her. She had Ryder to think about, and a tentative alliance with Robbie that could go up in flames at any moment. Her pairing up with a shifter wasn't going to make co-parenting with him any easier. Robbie was anti-shifter. Always had been. Always would be.

God, she'd messed up so badly with Robbie, and now she was making the same terrible mistake. Only this time, she didn't have the excuse of naïve youth, inexperience with men, or a shotgun wedding for freak's sake. She hadn't learned anything from the first time around, but had dove in beak first once again. And Mason didn't feel the same. He was hooked up on his ex and not ready to move on, and yet again, she was alone in this.

She had to get out of here.

Her stomach curdled and soured at the thought of leaving this place, these people, Mason. Today had felt good, freeing, and she'd owned who she was. She'd owned her inner animal right in front of Mason. But that wasn't enough to capture a man's heart, and she was in way over her head with this.

Affairs of the heart couldn't be trusted with someone whose heart had been fractured like mirror glass.

Beck shoved open the door to 1010. Maybe it was this old trailer's fault she'd fallen so unexpectedly hard. Cora had told her it was magic, and she hadn't listened. Instead, she'd gotten drunk on feeling a part of this place and clawed up Mason! He would never forgive her for doing that without his consent. Hell, she would never forgive herself.

Stupid owl thought she knew all the answers. She thought instinct trumped logic, but she didn't understand how the real world worked. Beck wasn't just an animal! She was a person, too, who'd just slashed an illegal claiming mark into the shoulder of a man she barely knew.

Facing Mason again couldn't happen. Not when she was this horrified by her reckless behavior. She would tell Cora something had come up and she needed to do her publicist duties from Saratoga, not from 1010, which was apparently akin to one of those cute little naked cupids shooting love arrows into everyone's asses.

She yanked her suitcase from the closet and rushed to the built-in set of drawers.

"Where are you going?" Mason asked.

"Aaah!" Beck screamed, clutching her chest as she spun on him.

He stood in the doorway, arms crossed over his chest, muscles bulging, eyes blazing a brilliant blue.

"I'm leaving," she squeaked out.

Mason blinked slow and raised his dark eyebrows. "Why?"

"Because I don't belong here! I don't have any control over my actions, which is insane because I'm a grown-ass woman. I've felt old and drained to emptiness for years, and then I come here and I'm making all these mistakes I can't afford to make. And I'm mortified by what I did to you."

Mason approached slowly, backing her into the corner as she countered him step for step. "What did you do to me?"

She couldn't breathe. Couldn't draw a single full breath into her lungs, and he was too close, too dominant, too riled up. A submissive snowy owl did not belong with a beast boar! Unable to force enough air past her voice box, she circled her finger in the general direction of the bloody tears in his shirt. When he stared at her like she'd lost her mind, she rasped out, "I marked you."

Mason shrugged flippantly and said, "Woman, it didn't hurt for more than a couple minutes, and it's already forming into a scar."

"How can you be so calm about this, Mason? It's a big deal! I never marked anyone before."

His face went completely slack as a spark of understanding lit up his eyes. Slowly, he dragged his gaze to his shoulder and pulled the tattered material to the side, exposing four perfect, deep, half-healed wounds. "You marked me? Like...*marked* me?" His voice jacked up in volume. "You claimed me?"

"I tried to stop my animal, I did, but I was angry, and my owl thought I was ruining things between us, and she really wants to keep you." Beck swallowed audibly and dropped her gaze to his scuffed work boots. Softly, she corrected herself, "*I* really want to keep you. I shouldn't have done that without talking to you about—"

Mason's lips crashed onto hers. The wind was knocked out of her, not because of his heavy dominance, but because he was squeezing her against his hard body.

Her back hit the wall hard, but she didn't care. She didn't feel the pain or have that trapped feeling anymore. Mason was touching her! More than touching her, he was giving into her completely!

His hands gripped her shirt roughly, and she tossed her head back and whispered his name as he ground his hard erection against her. His beard scratched at her sensitive skin as he dragged his lips down her neck and bit her hard. Not enough to draw blood, but hard enough that she felt his teeth sink into her skin by millimeters. "I didn't know," he rasped out as he pulled the backs of her knees up around his hips. "Boar people don't do claiming marks like that. I didn't even give a second thought to your talons on me, woman. Fuck, Beck, say it again. Tell me you claimed me."

"I claimed you," she chanted in a desperate murmur. "Mason," she groaned as the roll of his long, thick erection pressed her just right.

Mason settled her roughly on her feet, gripped her shirt, and then ripped it down the front, popping her buttons all over the laminate flooring. Desperately, she clawed his shirt upward and over his head, and the second he was free of the confining material, his lips were on her again.

Her breasts bounced to freedom as Mason yanked her bra off her arms. She raked her nails down his muscular chest, down the mounds of his taut abs. Damn, she'd never seen someone as perfect as him. Even the long scars on his ribs were sexy as hell. When she leaned forward and clamped her teeth against the raised scar, Mason hissed, then gripped her hair and pulled her in closer, as if he liked the pain. Rough, sexy, snarly beast. She'd had to carefully control her animal with Robbie and act submissive, but Mason could handle her appetites, and right now she wanted to feel him. She didn't want him gentle—not when both of their animals were riled up like this.

"I want you," she whimpered, fumbling with the fly of his jeans.

The rumble in his chest grew louder as he shoved his jeans down his hips, unsheathing his thick shaft. Just the weight of it when he pressed it against her belly made her knees buckle with longing. She'd never wanted a man like this. Never wanted to be filled like this. Sex had been about desperation to feel a connection before, but now, it felt like a vital link to touching Mason's soul. Is this what it was like to actually find a mate?

Gasping when his teeth found her neck again, she rolled her eyes closed and wiggled her hips, helping him shimmy her jeans down her legs. The second she was free of the fabric, their bodies crashed together, and she moaned at how damn good it felt to be pressed up against him. Warmth. Safety. Belonging. All the things she'd craved her entire life was right here for the taking.

Mason dropped sexy biting kisses to her breast, and worked her with that clever tongue of his until her sex pulsed once in delicious anticipation. God, she wanted him inside of her now.

But he had other ideas. Mason dropped to his knees, one hand on her breast, massaging with the perfect rough pressure as he sucked at the skin right over her pelvis, then lower and lower. By the time he pushed her knees wider apart, she was gripping his hair, guiding him, begging him, mewling out helpless pleading sounds. His teeth touched her left inner thigh, and then he clamped harder onto her right. Beck's knees gave out, but Mason gripped her shoulder in a blur, kept her pressed up against the wall. As she clenched his hair harder, the snarl in his throat sounded damn near like a purr, and the vibration touched her inner thigh. And when Mason looked up at her with those ice blue eyes and that wicked smile, she knew she was done for.

As punishment for his tease, she gripped the claiming mark so he would feel her. He winced, but his naughty smile grew wider. And the next time she rocked her hips toward him, he drew her clit into his mouth and just about buckled her over the erotic sensation.

And good gracious, that man knew how to draw an orgasm from her. He worked her into an inferno until she was loud, bowed back against the wall, hips rolling with the pace he set. And as if he knew she was right there, he slid his tongue deep inside of her. Three strokes, and she screamed his name as pulsing release drummed through her, more intense than she'd ever experienced before.

Mason stood, taking her with him, and tossed her on the soft mattress. He pushed her knees wide open as she lifted up to nip at his throat. And that big, dominant razorback boar shifter let her have his neck. If that didn't show complete trust, she didn't know what did.

Now her man wasn't playing around anymore. He wasn't readying her for his massive size or teasing. Up on locked, muscular arms, Mason settled into the cradle of her hips, trapped her in a fiery gaze, and slammed into her.

"Fuck," she gasped at how good he felt filling her like this.

Mason drew back slow, and then rammed into her again. He smoothed out his pace and bucked into her gracefully, keeping the pressure building in her middle until she was arching her spine against the bed, begging for more with her body.

"I'm gonna come again," she warned him breathlessly.

"Wait for me," he gritted out in a sexy, gravelly voice.

"I can't, I can't. Mason!"

He slammed into her faster, deeper. There was a strange feeling in her chest, as if Mason had touched her soul with a hot poker. She closed her eyes and gritted her teeth against the pleasure and pain. She knew what this was. It was exactly what had been missing with Robbie. Mason was bonding her to him, and after this she would never be the same. She wouldn't be able to leave and rip her heart away from him.

Mason winced, and she knew he felt it, too. Her mate. Hers.

He groaned out her name and froze as the first jet of warm seed pulsed into her, heating her from the inside out. She clawed at his back as her second orgasm slammed through her, even more intense than the first. She was falling…or flying. Weightless as pleasure pulsed through her body, warring with the ache in her chest, and then in an instant, the hurt was gone. Mason's dick throbbed inside of her as he emptied himself.

Lowering his weight on top of her, he slowed his pace and ground out her name. "Beck. My Beck." His voice sounded too low, too feral to pass as human, and she loved it. Loved this feeling he filled her with.

He moved inside of her until every last aftershock had subsided, and then he rolled over and cradled her to his chest. Mason's heartbeat drummed against her cheek, and Beck's face crumbled. Her eyes burned with tears because, God, it felt so good to be cared for. To not be used in the bedroom. To feel accepted and adored and coveted.

"Shhh." Mason stroked her hair, and his arm around her shoulders went gentle. He rubbed soothing circles right next to her spine, and his lips lingered in her hair.

Was that soft sob hers? Mortified, she squeezed her eyes closed and inhaled his scent, anchored herself in this moment as a tear streamed from the corner of her eye and made a tiny splat against the pillow.

"Please tell me these are happy tears," Mason murmured in a worried voice.

Beck drew her arms into his stomach and snuggled closer. Mason reacted immediately, hugging her up safe and warm in the circle of his strong arms.

Softly, so she wouldn't ruin the magic of this moment, she murmured, "I've been waiting all my life for you."

Mason's heartbeat raced faster, and he swallowed hard. When he spoke, there was a smile in his voice. "You've got me now, Beck. You run, I'll just follow. Beautiful, fierce… woman, you just drew my boar up and bound us."

"No, Mason." She smiled and laid a soft kiss against his chest, right over his heart. "We bound each other."

TWELVE

Mason had gone quiet beside her, tracing the vertebra in her spine as she lay relaxed on her belly. It wasn't an awkward silence, but the kind that was comfortable. It was the quiet that said he was as lost in this moment as she was.

As his gaze locked on hers, Mason's lips curved up in that slight smile he'd been giving her for the past half hour. He dragged his fingertip up her back to start at the top of her spine again.

Curiously, she asked, "What are you thinking about?"

He lowered his lips against her ear and whispered, "I never thought I would get a second chance at this feeling."

Fluffing the pillow up under her cheek, she said, "Claiming marks don't mean the same to boar people."

A frown marred his brows for a second before his face relaxed again. He shook his head and pressed his lips to her shoulder, then rested his cheek on his palm, elbow on the mattress. "I thought owl shifters were extinct."

"Very rare. Not extinct."

"Mmm," he rumbled in that sexy, deep timbre of his.

"Are there lots of boar shifters?"

Mason dipped his chin and traced her shoulder blade. "We number near a thousand."

"And you were supposed to rule them all?" She frowned. If she had other owls she could talk to and raise her child around, she would've done it, but as far as she knew, it was just her mom, Beck, and Ryder. "Why did you leave?"

The smile dipped from his lips, and his eyes went dark and serious. Mason lay on his arm right in front of her and searched her eyes. "Don't run."

"I won't. I just want to know you."

"We live in groups of ten to twenty called Drifts. Each is run by a dominant boar, but there is one Drift that governs the rest."

"That was your Drift?"

"My family's, yes. Bash was right about

boar people coveting money. We live well, and there is pressure to find high-paying jobs because paychecks are deposited into the same account for the good of the Drift. It is an honor to be an earner. To be able to provide for your Drift, as well as your mate and offspring." His eyes darkened with some emotion she didn't understand. "I was a very good earner. I had a brother, and we competed because, someday, we would battle for dominant boar over all our people. We had to excel in everything. To hold a top position, I had to be perfect. I had to have a high-paying job and a good mate who bore me offspring. Only I fell in love with an intern at the security company my family owned. I ran the company, had a good head for business, and I hired Esmerelda because my boar chose her the second she walked into my office for that interview." His eyes took on a faraway look. "She was beautiful. Dark hair, dark eyes, gorgeous Spanish accent. My human side had nothing to do with it, or I would've slowed us down."

"Why?"

"Because she was human, and boar shifters tend to stay together. I brought her into my Drift knowing she would be treated second-rate. My animal didn't care about that, though, because every woman I'd been raised around was strong. Tough. Thick-skinned. I assumed Esmerelda was the same." His lips pursed into a thin line before he murmured, "I was wrong. Her depression presented itself immediately. She swore it was seasonal and tried to hide her mood swings, but within the first few weeks we'd been mated, I got this sick feeling deep down that I couldn't make her happy. That nothing could. She started feeling the pressure of her station in our Drift. She was supposed to give me piglets and enable me to fight for the dominant boar position. She felt pressure to be perfect. She said having a baby would make her happier, so we tried. And tried and tried, and nothing happened. And the sows in my Drift were awful to her, because boar shifters procreate easily. Fertility problems are rare, and they blamed her for hurting my standing with our people. They wanted me to leave her, like I could just break the bond, and I started to hate them. My brother, Jamison, was the worst. He dug in, hounded her, because he could see hurting her was the best way to hurt me. He was after that dominant boar position, and our trouble conceiving gave him an edge because his mate was not only a sow, but she got pregnant right away. I was losing, but somewhere along the way, I stopped caring as much because I loved Esmerelda."

Heartbreak slashed through Mason's eyes as he ran the tip of his finger down Beck's cheek. "I worked a lot. My instinct to provide for Esmerelda and our future babies kicked up so hard, I couldn't stop pushing myself. More time at the office, more weekends ruined, and I couldn't see it, but Essie saw it as me pulling away from her. She couldn't understand shifter instincts because she wasn't one. I thought I was being a good mate, setting up a nest egg because I knew that someday we would get pregnant, but to her, she thought I resented her. She thought I was abandoning her. She was crying all the time. Arguing over nothing. She didn't want me to touch her. Stopped wanting to sleep with me. She would say, 'What's the point? I'm broken.' I didn't know what to do. I was twenty when we first paired up, young, stupid, head-strong, didn't understand depression, didn't understand her. She quit my company, didn't want to work, didn't want to get dressed, didn't want to brush her hair or go out or talk to people. I watched her wither. She became obsessed with these apple trees in our backyard. Just...babied them. Maybe they were her babies while we tried, I don't know. She was always out there with them, talking to them, pruning them, reading under their branches, obsessing over the fruit and any dead leaf. And one day, I came home from work dog tired, my Drift had been on my ass about offspring, had to fire someone that day, just in my own little world when I walked through the door. I couldn't wait to unload all my burdens on her because she always made me feel better. So I called her name, and when she didn't answer, I knew something was wrong. Just *knew it*." Mason's voice hitched, and he took a few seconds before he continued. "I found her in the backyard, hanging from one of the apple trees."

"Oh, my God," Beck murmured, pressing her hands over her mouth. "Mason."

"I went mad after that. Just..." Mason shook his head for a long time, and his eyes went hollow. "I didn't care about anything or anyone. I blamed my Drift for pushing her over the edge, but mostly I blamed myself for not knowing how to save her. My people started calling for me to prove myself if I still wanted to be in the running. I needed offspring, a mate, something. I was earning, but Jamison had pulled far ahead, and my dad wanted to step down as dominant boar. So he gave me two sows and told me to earn my keep."

Bile rose in Beck's throat. She hugged him tight and buried her face against his warm chest. She was a coward and couldn't watch the phantoms in his eyes anymore.

Mason's voice dipped to a ragged whisper. "I cared nothing for them. I just wanted Esmerelda back. But I'd stopped feeling somewhere along the way, and it was nice to escape into a rut and focus on breeding them just so I didn't have to think about how damned broken I was. So I didn't have to spend nights alone, listening to those goddamned apple trees creaking in the wind outside. By the end of that year, Jamison had me declared The Barrow. Rutting had made me weak. I hadn't been thinking about food, Changing, fighting, or anything. Just sex. Just this single-minded desperation to prove I wasn't worthless—for me, for Essie, for my Drift. I wasn't in any shape to fight and I knew it, but I went ahead and challenged Jamison just to put an end to all the pain. He was the only one who could match my boar. The only one who could send me to Essie with honor."

Beck's shoulders shook with her silent crying, and she gently traced the long scars up his ribs.

"Damon found me." Mason smoothed her hair from her face and hugged her close. "I was lying out in the woods, my people all around watching me bleed out. I'd been split open by Jamison's tusks, and I remember staring up at the stars, wondering why it was taking so damned long to die. And there was this wind, chaos and fire, and then everything went dark." Mason kissed her hairline and sighed. "And then I woke up in the dragon's lair, newly freed from my people."

"How did he find you?"

Mason shrugged. "I ask him that from time to time, and he just tells me he saved me because he was supposed to save me. The old dragon is full of riddles. I worked as a bodyguard, watching over his daughter, Diem, when she was in college as a favor to the man who had dragged me from the mud, and then when I came back here, I worked for him for different reasons."

"What reasons?"

Mason eased back and smiled sadly. "Because somewhere along the way, Damon became my friend. And even though he was quiet, reserved, and emotionless, I saw glimpses of the man he could be. I suspected he was just as broken as me, but I wanted to be there when the dragon rose again."

"And you were," she whispered, proud of Mason for overcoming such tragedy and turning into the incredible, loyal, strong, caring man he was today.

Mason ran his fingers through her hair and agreed. "And I was."

"Can I tell you a secret?" she asked.

"I want to know all your secrets."

Beck drew his knuckles to her lips and laid a soft peck on his skin. "None of that made me want to run." She wiped her damp cheek on the pillow and braved a look in his eyes. "It only made me like you more."

THIRTEEN

Beep, beep, beep, beep!

Beck cracked her eye open just in time to watch Mason's giant hand arch through the air and smash the alarm clock into tiny pieces. The poor contraption made a pathetic last attempt to wake them with a strangled *beeeeeep*, but then died completely, the glowing green *6:00 am* fading to darkness.

Beck pursed her lips to hide her shocked laugh. Apparently Mason wasn't fully awake. She could tell by the fact that he dragged her body closer to his chest, big-spooned her like a pro, and told her, "I'll keep you safe, babe."

From the alarm clock?

Beck turned in his arms and buried her face against his chest, then inhaled his scent. He smelled different when he slept, more like Mason and less like the manly sexpot body spray he used in the mornings. And she freaking loved that she was the one who got to experience this. *Mine, mine, mine,* her owl hooted possessively.

Mason lifted his powerful leg over her hips and trapped her in his embrace completely, and this right here was her favorite place in the world. Partly because she was pretty sure it was impossible to feel safer than in his big, muscly arms, and two, he had some serious morning wood that conjured all the fun memories of last night.

Beck wished she could stay in bed with him longer. It was summer, but nights were still cool in the mountains, and he was like a big sexy furnace. She had to get ready for the long day ahead though. The more she fell for Mason, the more determined she was to help the shifters—not just for her and Ryder's future, but for the future of Damon's mountains and the incredible people here, too. She'd been here almost a week and had managed to meet with all the crews here thanks to Bash being happy to drive her after Mason had quit. She loved them all—the Ashe Crew, the Gray Backs, the Boarlanders, Damon and his beautiful family. She'd even met Kong's Lowlander family group in Saratoga when she'd done a grocery run with Audrey. Her heart was throwing out lifelines to each crew, each member, tethering her here to this place. How silly that she'd thought she could leave, like her time here had meant nothing. She was changed. She was stronger somehow, which was insane because she'd always been proud of her toughness, but these people here made her want to get battle-ready. They made her career more than just a job. They made it fulfilling, but only if she succeeded in helping them.

Everyone had a role to play here. The mates that had been brought into the Boarlanders didn't sit idly by and watch their men defend themselves alone. Audrey was in town every chance she got, being friendly, signing autographs, because the white tiger she hid inside was also rare. And Bash's mate, Emerson, was writing pro-shifter first-person articles full-time for the *Saratoga Hometown News*. And on top of that, she hadn't balked an inch when Beck had asked her to write blogs for Cora's website and open a forum on the bangaboarlander page. Already they were getting a great response from the public who were curious about life in Damon's mountains. And Kirk's mate, Alison, who had asked Beck to call her Ally, had made ballsy moves with a video interview that made international news. She had silenced IESA completely after they tried to kill her a couple months ago. Her outspoken and public vitriol for the rogue government group had civilians picketing and raging against the injustices done to the shifters.

It was time Beck stepped up and pulled her weight, too.

Beck laid a kiss on her mate's chest, hugged him tighter, then wiggled out from under his heavy arm and leg. His hand clamped on hers the second her feet hit the cold floorboard.

"Nooo," he drawled softly. "It's too early."

She giggled and pulled her hair into a high messy bun. "The early bird gets the worm."

"Mmm. That statement right there would break Willa's heart."

Beck laughed. Oh, she'd met the worm-lovin' Almost Alpha of the Gray Backs. "The photographer for the calendar will be here soon, and I need to get ready."

"How soon?"

"Forty-five minutes."

A naughty smile stretched Mason's lips. He pulled her back into bed and over him until she straddled his hips. His lightened gaze dipped to her bare breasts, and he ran his hands up her ribs, then lifted his shoulders up off the bed and drew one of her nipples into his mouth. As he laved his tongue against her sensitive skin, Beck closed her eyes and arched her back, encouraging him.

Mason relaxed back and rolled his hips under her. "You're sensitive, woman. You come easy for me."

"Your point?"

Mason sat up again and cupped the back of her neck, laid a nipping kiss at the base of her throat. "I could have you in five," he murmured.

Beck gave a private grin at the headboard behind him because, damn, she should really be getting ready, but that was one helluva pretty offer from her man. Teasingly, she lowered her lips to his ear and whispered, "Or I'll have you in five." Slowly, she lifted off his hips and positioned herself right over the head of his hard cock.

She slid over him slow and easy, then pulled off him quick. Down slow, up quick, and Mason's hips jerked as a soft rumble vibrated in his chest. Big, powerful man, allowing her the dominant position in their bed. Mason's arms wrapped around her back, and he pulled her closer, buried his face at her neck as she gripped the back of his hair and lost herself in the erotic friction they were creating in the first rays of dawn light that filtered in through the window blinds.

When her skin chilled from the sensations taking over her body, Mason pulled the blanket to her back as if his instincts had told him exactly what she needed. Beck rolled her hips faster as the pressure built between her legs, and Mason drew his knees up, cradling her as their bodies crashed against each other. Her insides tingled, and the pressure was too much. She threw her head back and cried out as she came. By the second pulse of her orgasm, Mason clutched her hard and went rigid, growled out her name. His shaft throbbed as he shot warmth into her. God, she loved this. Loved him filling her. Loved this connection. Loved his instant reaction to her body. Loved him.

Loved him?

She slowed the pace as it hit her that this was something monumental. She'd accepted she would live a life void of love from a mate, but here she was, giving her heart to someone who was worthy. To someone she could trust with it.

"I love you," she whispered against his ear, too scared to look in his eyes when she admitted it out loud.

Another deep pulse from Mason's dick, and he relaxed. Easing back, he lifted those beautiful inhuman eyes to hers. Honesty pooled there as he smiled and said, "I love you, too."

"Really?" Beck said, chest heaving with emotion.

Mason drew her into his strong embrace and rocked them slowly from side to side. He rubbed her back gently and said, "Yeah, really, but I was planning on telling you first."

"Competitive," she accused him through a laugh.

"Nah, I just had it in my mind that I was going to take you out and tell you at a nice dinner. Make it special. But you know what?"

"What?" she asked, squeezing his shoulders tight. She couldn't believe he was really hers, and that she wasn't dreaming this.

"Your way was better."

"Naturally."

Mason tickled her ribs and asked, "Naturally? Woman, that's cocky."

She was giggling hard now because he'd

found her most ticklish place on her stomach and had dug in. "You're the cocky one now. Stop it, you monster."

"Mmm, I'm *your* monster, though," he rumbled, flipping her over and pulling her beside him on the bed. "Five more minutes."

"No! I only have forty minutes to get ready now, and I have to look professional today."

Mason was nibbling at the back of her neck with those sexy nipping teeth of his. And oooh, now he was sucking on her, and the pull of her skin between his lips made her arch her ass against him instinctively. His grip on her waist was hard as he angled her farther back against him.

"Mason!" she yelped. He was getting riled up again, and as fun as it sounded to fool around with him all day, she really had to stop them at some point. Beck abandoned the covers and scrambled from bed.

Mason grabbed for her backside and missed, then grunted and lay limp, half off the bed with a sexy little pout on his bottom lip. She couldn't help the giggles that bubbled up her throat. "You owe me an alarm clock, by the way."

Mason frowned at the destroyed appliance.

Beck bustled into the bathroom and called out, "And also breakfast since it's your fault I'm running late!"

FOURTEEN

"Clinton, for the last time, I'm begging you...just take off the gym socks." Eight in the morning, and Beck was already about done with this day thanks to the ridiculous man standing before her.

Clinton had done everything she'd asked: fixed his sandy colored hair into a stylish mess on top of his head, trimmed his facial scruff so it looked designer, and he'd even cleaned and polished both his chainsaw and his brand new white Ford Raptor, which she was pretty sure he bought just to compete with Mason's truck. He'd started testing her with the jeans she'd asked him to wear, though. She'd said "sexy, with well-placed holes," and Clinton had decided on redneck lookin' cut-off jean shorts with a hole in his crotch that clearly showed his dick. And then to top off his look, a pair of atrocious yellow and white knee-high gym socks clung to his hairy legs. If the smile he was wearing was anything to go by, this had been the plan since he'd made the deal to take a picture for the calendar.

"Can we edit the socks out?" Beck asked the photographer, a sweet, mousy woman named Drea.

"It would be easier to just add jeans to him later."

"No!" Clinton barked as he hit another ridiculous pose. He held his chainsaw up in the air, splayed his legs and yep, his giant dick flopped right out of the hole in his jean shorts. "Are you getting this one? This one will sell millions." He was trying to contain his laughter, and Beck wanted to claw that stupid smile right off his stupid face.

Behind her, Harrison, Bash, and Kirk were chuckling, and it was all too much.

"This is shoot one out of twelve today. Twelve! And already we've wasted an hour staring at your dick!"

"Hey, I manscaped it, just like you asked!" Clinton yelled.

"I meant your chest, *Clinton*," she gritted out. "This isn't an R-rated calendar. Harrison," she pleaded, turning to the alpha, "can you talk to him? Please."

"Oh, no." Harrison's blue eyes sparked with amusement. "I don't have any control over that asshole. I'm fine sitting back and watching someone else try to handle him for a while. Not my circus, not my monkeys."

She let off a screech that sounded like nails on a chalkboard. This was just great that Clinton was already working up her animal.

"Hey, you're eyes are pee-pee yellow." Clinton pelvic-thrusted and revved the chainsaw up in the air, waggling his eyebrows not-so-seductively, and she wanted to kick everything.

The photographer stopped clicking away on her digital camera with the long lens and arched her eyebrow at the images she reviewed. "I mean...we'd have to cut half of him out of the pictures. There's not really a good angle for the shape we need for the calendar."

Beck turned her hands into little claws as she gripped her daily planner to her chest. With a frozen, feral smile for Clinton, she said too shrilly, "It's okay. Everything is okay. Clinton, you're out of the calendar!" *There, take that, ass.*

"Finally," Clinton muttered. He lowered

the chainsaw to the ground and hooked his hands on his hips. And then, dick out, he said, "Anyone want to get drunk and eat pizza rolls up at Bear Trap Falls with me?"

Bash raised his hand like he was a giant school boy. "Well, I want to—"

"No!" Beck hollered. "No, no, no. Clinton, you can go do whatever you want. You three are coming with me."

"But"—Bash pouted—"he's making pizza rolls."

Harrison was grinning like this was the funniest thing he'd seen in his life, Kirk was laying on the ground, hands linked behind his head and definitely snoring, and Bash was now asking, "When's lunch?"

"It's eight in the morning, Bash. Didn't you just have breakfast?"

Bash shrugged like that was a silly question. "Yeah, *first* breakfast."

Beck blinked hard, shook her head, counted to three, and opened her daily planner again. "Bash," she said, forcing a calm voice, "you're up next. Your setting is the Boarlander woods. Somewhere pretty and mossy with lots of shade. Do you know a place that is close?"

Bash pointed to the tree line behind the

trailers, twenty yards away. "That's good."

Clinton had sucked the wind straight out of her sails, so Beck sighed and said, "Great."

She marched toward the woods, leading the others, and let Drea have the reins on Bash since he was much more open to direction. And while the behemoth was rubbing moisturizer over his rippling muscles, Beck let off a little sound of relief. Bash would take a better picture and not give her the mountainous pile of shit Clinton had.

And now she had to figure out an extra picture since she'd been depending on Clinton for January. She'd spent hours sketching out ideas and imagining how this would go, and in all the time she'd worked on this project, losing their first model right out of the gate hadn't even crossed her mind.

She shook her head as she looked over the list of months.

January – ~~Clinton, bear, Boarlander~~
February – Bash, bear, Boarlander
March – Harrison, bear, alpha of the Boarlanders
April – Kirk, silverback, Boarlander
May – Creed, bear, alpha of the Gray Backs
June – Matt, bear, Gray Back
July – Beaston, bear, Gray Back

August – Tagan, bear, alpha of the Ashe Crew

September – Haydan, bear, Ashe Crew

October – Bruiser, bear, Ashe Crew

November – Brighton and Denison, twin bears, requested shoot together, Ashe Crew

December – Damon, dragon, king of the motherfuckin' mountains

Meet Robbie tonight at Sammy's, 9:00

"Crap," she muttered. She'd been so caught up in everything here, she'd completely forgotten about her meeting with McFartFace. Irritated, she scribbled devil horns on Robbie's name while she tried to work through who she would shoot for January. Everyone on her list was all the ones who had agreed to be in the calendar. Everyone else was a hard no. And she couldn't split up the Beck brothers or they would bow out of the project. Theirs was going to be a music shoot with their guitars. Still shirtless and sexy, but their fans would be ravenous for a spread of both of them together.

"Hey," Mason murmured right beside her ear.

"Aaah!" Beck yelped, jumping nearly out of

her skin.

Mason backed away, barely saving the trio of coffees in his hands from spilling, a big old grin on his face. On his beautiful, shaven face.

"Mother of pearl," she murmured as she dragged her gaze along his clean-shaven jawline. Dark eyes said his animal was content, a straight, strong nose, sensual lips lifted in a smile, and his chiseled jawline belonged on a model. And the deeper his smile grew, the deeper two sexpot dimples became.

"Beck."

She wanted to swim in those dimples. She wanted to dive into them and backstroke around in them, then snuggle up and take a nap and wake up and squish her cheek against the sides of her dimple bed...

"Beck?" Mason said again, looking concerned now. "Are you okay?"

Will you marry me? Stop it. Breathe and stop being weird. He looks worried. Say something smart. "I saw Clinton's dick." *Freaking perfect.*

Mason's dark eyebrows lifted slightly. "Everyone has seen Clinton's dick. He's real proud of it."

"Mine's bigger," Bash called from where Drea was positioning him against a tree.

"Y-your ummm," Beck stammered, gesturing to Mason's perfect jawline and lips. "Your face is my favorite."

"It's my favorite, too," Bash chimed in.

The worry in Mason's eyes morphed to amusement, and was that a blush in his cheeks? "I roughed up your face last night and felt bad. Figured I'd shave for you so you don't have to flinch away when we're kissing."

So he planned on more kissing! Eeeee! Beck cleared her throat coolly and murmured, "I really appreciate it. I loved you bearded, but this…" She lifted her fingertips to his face, hesitated for a moment, then brushed a light touch down his cheek. "This is a good surprise."

Mason pressed her hand against against his jaw, nuzzled her palm, then laid a soft kiss on her wrist. "I brought coffee. Figured you could use it after all the not-sleeping we did last night."

She giggled, deliriously happy now that her mate was here. *Her mate*. God, she couldn't believe this was happening. "Three coffees?"

"One for me and you, and one for the photographer willing to put up with the shit she's gonna have to deal with today. I hope you're paying her well."

"I am. Cora Keller hired her with the budget from donations that have been pouring into her site. She's also been selling shifter T-shirts, mugs, pens, hats, the works to raise money."

"That woman is amazing."

"She really is. She has all the Breck Crew working around the clock to help with PR, but she didn't have enough pull here."

"And that's where you came in," Mason said proudly, handing her a fancy disposable coffee cup with a lid.

"Yep," she said, taking a burning sip of the delicious wakey-wakey nectar. "Ooooh, heaven. Drea, coffee is here when you want it."

"Thanks, Beck," Drea said, reviewing shots she'd just taken of Bash.

Emerson was here now, pregnant belly pushing against her T-shirt as she plucked a fuzz off Bash's dark facial scruff. And if her ears were on point, she could hear Audrey and Ally talking and giggling and headed this way to help. Today was about to get easier with their back-up.

Bash turned with a grin and said something low in Emerson's ear, cupped her belly affectionately, his tall stature as strong as the tree he stood next to, muscles flexed as he talked to his mate.

"Drea," Beck whispered, then jerked her chin at the couple.

"You want some candid shots?" Drea asked through a spreading grin.

"Yeah."

Drea didn't have to be asked twice. Immediately, she began snapping pictures of Bash cradling Emerson's belly. Emerson was laughing, her hands on Bash's chest like they were the only ones out in these woods.

An unexpected emotion washed over Beck as she watched them, and she rested her hand on her chest to stop the fluttering.

"What's wrong," Mason asked, resting his fingertips on her lower back.

"Nothing. They're beautiful."

Mason frowned from her to Bash and Emerson, and then back to Beck. "You never had that, did you?"

She smiled through her emotions. Unable to speak, she shook her head. Robbie hadn't been happy over the news that she'd become pregnant. Wasn't happy with their shotgun wedding. Wasn't happy with her.

Mason pressed his hand on her stomach and lowered his lips to her ear. "If I was there, it would've been different. I would've taken care of you. I hate that I missed it. I saw your stretch marks last night, and it gutted me that I wasn't there when you got them. I'm sorry I can't give you that."

"You silly man. Don't apologize for stuff neither one of us can control." She swallowed hard and rested her cheek against his chest. "And thanks for being nice about my stretch marks. I used to be really self-conscious about them."

"Because of Robbie?"

A nod of her head was all he would get. She couldn't bring herself to voice the pain she'd felt time and again at Robbie's revulsion of her body after she'd had Ryder.

"I love them," he admitted low. "I'm not just saying that either. If this is all I get from you being pregnant, it's enough." Mason brushed his finger up under her shirt and across the marred skin right near her hip. "Warrior stripes."

She laughed thickly and lifted up on her toes, kissed him and reveled in the smoothness of his face. Easting away, she promised, "Now we're gonna be making out all the time."

Mason pumped his fist and murmured, "Yes, woman."

They watched Bash's shoot for a while before Mason asked, "How did Clinton's shoot go?"

"I have a feeling you already know."

"That bad?"

"I'm having to cut him, and now I don't know who to get for January. I already had to beg a couple of the Ashe Crew to participate."

"I'll do it."

She bumped his shoulder and shook her head. "You can't, Mason. You've kept your existence here a secret for a long time, and for a reason. You don't want your boar-people finding you, and neither do I."

"Nah, I have an idea that will keep me out of the calendar but get you your January shot."

"What idea?"

Mason's eyes crinkled with his wicked grin. "Clinton's easier when he drinks, and he's hitting the whiskey hard right now. And also, he's competitive. Just have your photographer ready for whatever he gives you."

****

"What is he doing?" Drea asked as Mason pulled his black Raptor right up next to Clinton's white one.

"I think he's luring one hard-headed little bee to some honey too sweet to ignore," Kirk answered behind Beck.

Huh. Beck settled in behind Drea, who was changing out the lens on her camera. Mason revved his roaring engine, then got out of his truck.

Clinton's screen door screeched open, and he stuck his head out, narrowed his eyes at Mason's truck, then retreated back inside. A second later, the blinds on his front window lifted.

Beck hid her grin as the Boarlanders chuckled behind her. Oooh, Mason knew just what he was doing.

Mason peeled out of his shirt, and Beck's face went slack. His eight-pack rippled with his movement, and his scars stood stark on his skin. His biceps bulged as he wadded up his T-shirt and tossed it out of the way. And when he lifted his gaze to Beck, his eyes were blazing the bright blue of his boar people. Harrison tossed him a hard hat, which Mason caught easily.

"He needs moisturizer," Audrey said matter-of-factly. She plopped a tube of it into Beck's hand, slapped her on the ass, and said, "You should do the honors."

As Beck stumbled forward, Bash chortled behind her. "Mason's gonna get a boner so bad."

She was going to lose it right here in front of everyone. Already her owl was screeching for her to hurry up and get closer to her mate. To touch him. To splay her fingers across his taut chest, lick him, unbutton his pants, and...*focus*.

Mason lifted his chin proudly, watched her approach with those gorgeous glowing blues. "I like your eyes when your animal is ruffled. Not gold like I thought in the restaurant, but they're yellow like the sun. Hard to look at, hard to look away." He caught her hand as she lifted lotion up to his chest. Lowering his voice to a barely audible whisper, he said, "They're captivating." Slowly, he drew her hand to his chest and rolled his eyes closed when she touched him.

"Boner!" Bash said. "I shoulda made a bet. It smells like pheromones."

"That's good, Bash Bear," Emerson said through a giggle.

"What's that on your shoulder?" Harrison asked.

Beck froze at the realization of what Mason had exposed by losing his shirt. Her healing claiming mark was still red and angry looking on his shoulder. Four long, deep gashes stretched across his shoulder where she'd marked him with her razor sharp talons in a fit of lust and insanity.

"Nothing," she blurted out.

"Or everything," Mason said, cocky-as-you-like. "My girl laid into me and gave it to me. I'm claimed, boys."

"Aw, hell yeah!" Kirk whooped as the others cheered and whistled. "Well, show us yours then, Beck!"

"Uuuh," she said, frowning at Mason's mark. Her cheeks flushed with heat as she turned slowly. What was she supposed to say that wouldn't mortify her?

"She doesn't have one," Mason murmured. The humor had been sucked right out of his tone.

The cheering died down to silence so heavy it made it hard to breathe. Her face was on fire now as she dropped her gaze to the ground. Mason had said claiming was different for his people, but the Boarlanders apparently thought she was supposed to have one. And now her old insecurities were rearing their ugly heads.

Drea snapped a picture, but Beck didn't want that. She didn't want the shame on her face captured for all eternity in a photograph, so she handed Mason the moisturizer and ducked out of the way of his grasping hand.

"Beck—"

"Nope," she gritted out, not about to do this in front of the whole damned crew.

"You're doin' it all wrong," Clinton said from beside his truck. Now he was dressed in low-riding jeans and work boots, and he had his chainsaw in hand again. With a scowl, the grumpy Boarlander drew up in front of the grill of his pickup, lifted his chainsaw, splayed his legs, flexed his abs deep, lifted his chin, and gave Drea the money shot.

"Got it," Drea said excitedly as she snapped pictures in quick succession. And when she looked back at her camera to review, she had that big grin that said Clinton's picture was done.

Clinton gave Mason a middle finger plus one cocky smirk, then sauntered back into this trailer.

Mason didn't seem to give a single fuck, though. His eyes were somber and steady on Beck. Regret swam there, and she didn't even want to know why. God, how stupid that she'd done it again. She'd believed him when he'd said claiming was different for his people. She'd assumed there was some ceremony or something that she would soon be a part of, but there wasn't. The Boarlanders' confusion over her not bearing Mason's mark said his traditions were the same as other shifters, and Beck had gone and fallen for his pretty words.

She'd picked Mason.

Apparently, he hadn't picked her back.

FIFTEEN

Beck looked at the picture of Damon standing in front of the waterfall next to his cliff mansion. His white oxford shirt was unbuttoned to expose one seriously ripped set of abs, his eyes sliver, his pupils elongated, chin lifted, and that sexy smirk on his lips. It was the perfect picture to end on.

"December is done. Great job everyone," Beck declared. "That's a wrap!"

Cheering erupted behind her at a deafening level. They'd attracted the shifters as they'd gone from crew to crew, taking photos of the most dominant beasts of these mountains. Excitement had built as more and more of the shifters and their mates and children had come out to show support. And now, as she looked around, Beck was stunned to realize almost everyone was here. The Ashe crew, led by Tagan and his mate Brooke, were laughing and cutting up with Creed's Gray Backs and Harrison's Boarlanders. Damon and his mate Clara, who was holding their red-headed toddler, made their way to where Beaston was standing with his mate, Aviana, mooning over their beautiful baby raven boy. Willa was cracking jokes and cradling a cardboard container of what she described as her "baby worms," and beside her Drea was snapping candid pictures of everyone.

Beck was the only one on the outside looking in.

Silly her. She'd thought for a moment she was a part of this, but she'd been mistaken. She was here for a job, and Mason was broken enough that she had entertained him for a while. But not enough to commit to her, as her animal had demanded she do.

"I'll send you everything I have and put together the calendar as soon as I get these photos edited," Drea said distractedly. "It'll probably be a week before I get you any of the files."

"That would be perfect," Beck said softly. "Thanks so much for doing this. The pictures I saw are incredible."

"Thanks. I'm pro-shifter, so this was really

a dream job. I mean, who gets to meet and photograph the shifters in Damon's mountains? Don't worry about me, though. As per our contract, I will only share these pictures with you, and I'll give you all the files as soon as we send the calendar to the printer."

"Great." Beck shook Drea's hand. "It was a pleasure working with you."

"The pleasure is mine. You have a real good thing going up here."

Beck's heart felt like it was being run through with hot metal, but she resisted the urge to wince at the pain as she made her way down to where all the trucks, cars, and jeeps were parked in Damon's yard. She hopped over a long scorch mark. Her instincts told her she didn't want anything to do with the bad mojo wafting from it.

"Can we talk?" Mason asked from where he was leaning against his truck.

Beck startled to a stop. She had thought he'd shoved off when she'd left for the Grayland Mobile Park to shoot the Gray Backs.

Beck checked her watch. "Sorry, but I don't have time to hash this out right now. It's getting late, and I have a long drive to Saratoga. Bash said I could borrow his ride."

She dangled the fun-lovin' bear's keys up in the air as proof.

"Are you going to meet Robbie?"

That was none of his damned business. Beck bustled past him and yanked open the door to Bash's truck, but Mason plucked the keys from her hand, tossed them in the passenger's seat, and threw her over his shoulder like a sack of mulch.

"Dammit, Mason. Put me down!" She beat on his back, but he didn't even flinch under her.

"You're being stubborn and, besides, Bash needs his ride. I'm your driver, so I'll be the one taking you to meet your ex." With a grunt, he set her in the front seat of his Raptor and slammed the door.

He blurred around the front of the truck before she could scramble out. The truck rocked as he slid in and shut his door. "And after we go meet your baby-daddy, I'm taking you out."

"No, thank you. I can only handle managing one bad decision at a time. Not two."

He leveled her with a look so intense she couldn't hold his gaze. "Don't you call me a bad decision, woman."

He spun out of the yard and blasted down

Damon's well-paved road.

"Why were the Boarlanders so surprised by you not claiming me?"

Mason made a pissed-off ticking sound behind his teeth and turned down the blaring radio. "Because they don't understand what I'm going through. I don't talk about it with them. If I was okay right now, things would be different, but as it stands, I'm not ready to mark you."

"Why not?" she asked softly.

Mason shook his head for a long time, jaw clenched hard. "Because of Esmerelda. Because I'm just not ready."

"How long ago did she pass?"

"Beck," he warned.

"How long ago, Mason? It's not a hard question!"

"Ten years. She hung herself ten years ago."

A decade. Beck felt slapped and socked in the stomach all at once. "Mason, I've been split up with Robbie for a few years, and I was ready enough to mark you because I really do love you. Because my animal chose you. If you're still hanging on that hard to Esmerelda...if I'm not pulling at your claiming instincts after so much time without a mate…maybe I'm not it for you."

Mason looked sick as he whispered, "Beck, it's just not that simple."

"It really is. I don't want to be a replacement mate that you keep around because I'm comfortable. I don't want to compete with a ghost. I don't want to play second fiddle. I did that before with Robbie. I played replacement pussy for him every time he came home from one of his girlfriends, and it gutted me. It ruined my heart. I had no self-worth, didn't value myself at all, I hurt all the time. I can't do that again."

"It won't be like that if you can just give me time to get myself out of the hole I've dug."

"You mean the hole Esmerelda dug."

"Yeah, Beck. We should be taking this slower. I haven't even met your kid yet. I don't know if I'll be any good at parenting or at being a mate for you. I screwed up everything when I was with my first mate. She's dead because I couldn't make her happy. A claiming mark came easy for you, but for me, I want to be careful. I want to make sure I do this clear-headed when I'm not spiraling. I want to make sure it keeps and I can make you happy before I bond us like that."

"You already bonded us, Mason! Last night,

did you not feel it? Did you not feel the painful pull to me when we were making love? You carved your name into my soul. Did I not do that to yours?"

No answer.

"Mason, tell me if it's not the same for you. Please."

"Did you mark Robbie?" he asked in a strangled voice.

She drew back in shock at his question. "No. I wanted to when Ryder was born, but I couldn't. My animal wouldn't let me claim a man who wasn't my mate and, thank God, because I suffered enough rejection from that man. Breaking a bond would've killed me."

"Yeah," Mason rasped out. He cast her a quick glance, then dragged his eyes back to the road. "Esmerelda was my mate, and we were bound. It took me ten years to move on from the pain of her loss. Hell, I'm still hurting. I just want to make sure I never have to break a bond with you, too. I'm just asking for time."

Loaded moments dragged on between them as she stared at his profile. He really wasn't hers. Not like she'd thought. "You can take all the time you need."

Before he could respond, she turned up the radio and gave her attention to the piney woods that blurred past her window. Any more rejection, and she would cry. And right now, she didn't feel like sharing grief with any man, especially not one who had chipped away at her icy heart and made her vulnerable again. How dare he? She'd gotten so strong, so hardened, and he'd come along and ripped her defenses down. Now she was bleeding and raw again.

He'd given her hope for a different life. One where she wasn't limping from day to day, alone in raising her child, sequestered away from other shifters, watching her rights and the rights of her son stripped away one by one. For a blinding, beautiful second, she'd imagined raising Ryder here with other shifter kids and families who supported what she was trying to do instead of a stupid ex who shamed her for the owl that lived inside of her. She'd dreamed of a life with Mason, trailer park and all, because he made her feel alive for the first time in so long. She had begun to think she deserved better than all the shit Robbie had put on her.

A tear streaked from the corner of her eye, but quick as a whip, she dashed it away. Clasping her hands in her lap, she blew out a long, steadying breath and collected herself.

She had to mentally prepare to deal with Robbie, and right now, she had no room for her insecurities with Mason.

She would get through this, just like she did everything else. Alone.

Why? Because she was a fighter. And if Mason couldn't see past his first mate to Beck's value, then okay.

The problem with ghosts was it was easy to remember the good. It was easy to forget the bad when a broken heart wanted to cling to the happy, devoted memories.

The problem with ghosts was they weren't around to remind the living of their imperfections.

If Mason wasn't capable of letting Esmerelda go, Beck would just have to find her happiness elsewhere.

SIXTEEN

"I feel like you're pulling away from me," Mason said as he skidded to a stop in the parking lot of Sammy's Bar.

Beck's silence had slowly crippled him on the drive here. He'd hurt her again. He couldn't seem to stop hurting her, an unfortunate byproduct of both of their baggage.

Beck had withered in the seat next to him, and now she sat there, avoiding his gaze, arms crossed over her chest like armor. Against him? Fuck.

He was trying to do this right. Claiming her when he was still spiraling over the death of another mate wasn't fair to Beck. She deserved all of his heart, all of his attention.

Beck deserved all of him.

He could only imagine how she felt right now. Rejected, likely, but if she could only see how devoted to her he was already, maybe she would give him some slack. But Beck had been cheated on, time and time again, and she was at a point in her life where she wanted to be the top priority for a man. Good on her. She'd just picked Mason at the wrong time.

Wrong time? Her expression when he'd told her Essie had died ten years ago flashed across his mind. She'd been shocked that his first mate was still such a big part of his life after so long, he could tell. And maybe she was right.

Mason swallowed hard and slid his hand over her tense thigh. "Ten years is a long time to mourn. I know that, but it passed so quickly. It was like I sleepwalked through my life here in Damon's mountains. I worked, ate, thought about how I'd screwed up her life, slept, and did it all again, day after day. And somewhere along the line, I forgot how to smile and breathe and feel, and then you came along and reminded me that I'm not dead yet."

He tucked her red-gold hair behind her ear to see her face, but her eyes were closed and her bottom lip trembling, and God, he was breaking inside for what he was doing to her.

"I don't want to be a reminder to live, Mason," she whispered. "I want to be the one you choose. People come into your life for different reasons. Some are there to push you to become better or to teach you a lesson. But a few come in because they can give you honest-to-goodness, undiluted happiness, and they're supposed to stay there." She lifted tear-rimmed seafoam green eyes to his, and her voice trembled with honesty when she admitted, "I was hoping to be the one who stayed."

"Babe," he murmured, pulling her over onto his lap. She allowed it, so he cupped her cheeks and searched her eyes. "You are. Just because I didn't give you a claiming mark the same day you gave me one doesn't mean it isn't on my mind. It doesn't mean this thing between us is less-than. But I'm seeing Esmerelda. I'm hearing her, too. I'm haunted right now, and I don't want to do this and you look back on this time and think you were a reaction. You're no one's reaction, Beck. You deserve your own time without Esmerelda's ghost fuckin' with my head. Now, I haven't seen or heard from her since you put this mark on me, and Beck, that mark means the world to me. I'm in this, even if I'm waiting a minute to mark you back. But I want to make sure she's gone for good, okay?"

"Robbie always said—"

"Fuck what your ex said. I'm not him, and I won't be paying for his mistakes either, just like I won't make you pay for Esmerelda's mistakes. This is me and you, and I'm fighting to let my ghost go. You have to let yours go, too."

Beck dropped her gaze, and a heartbreaking little tear slipped down her cheek. He wiped it off with the pad of his thumb and angled her face up, locked their gazes. "You can trust me, Beck. I'm right here with you, okay?"

God, she was so beautiful, face open and raw, cheeks flushed, looking at him like she was so scared he would let her down. He wouldn't. Mason was going to do everything in his power to make sure she never felt unworthy again. "Okay?" he whispered again.

She nodded and slid her arms around him, hugged him tight, and buried her face against his neck and, fuck, he wanted to take her here. He wanted to make her come slow, make her feel how much he loved her because, over the course of the day, she'd forgotten. She didn't know it, and he wouldn't bring up any more women with her when she was so hurt over Essie, but he hadn't been with anyone since those two sows he'd failed to get pregnant. It had been a long damn time since he'd let himself open up to a woman like this. Beck was his, and he was hers in ways he couldn't explain to her without rubbing salt in her open wounds.

He gripped her hair gently and pulled her close, stared at the neon green Sammy's sign over her shoulder and sighed. And now with all that hurt churning inside her, she was going to have to face her ex. This sucked. He wished he could take care of this part for her, but co-parenting with Robbie was solely on Beck's shoulders.

The clock changed to *9:00*, so Mason kissed her forehead, let his lips linger there, and then eased back. "Do you want me to come in with you?"

Beck looked uncertain. "I think so. Robbie brought his girlfriend Shelly to me when they got serious since she would be in Ryder's life. I guess Robbie needs to meet you, too, so he doesn't feel disrespected. But then, I don't know where you and I stand—"

"Mark or no, you're my mate, and I'm yours."

Her full lips trembled into a smile. "Okay. Maybe give me some distance so I can work my way up to introducing you. Robbie doesn't do well with surprises. I need to prep him first."

"Sounds good. Whatever you need."

Beck moved to escape his lap, but hesitated. "Oh, and your instincts will probably tell you to stab him." She scrunched up her nose. "Try not to."

Mason chuckled and squeezed her ass, just because he needed the weight of it in his hand for reassurance before he went in and met her ex. "I have complete control over my temper."

****

Mason did not have control over his temper. If he gripped his pool stick any harder, he was going to break it into splinters. Beck tried to ignore yet another dirty look he tossed at the back of Robbie's head as her ex bitched about how she'd been late. If she didn't hurry Robbie's visit up, Mason was going walk over to their table and gouge her ex's eyes out, probably with a smile on his face. At least Robbie hadn't noticed Mason yet, because if he had, he would be complaining about that and not the time.

"Robbie, I don't know what to tell you. You said nine o'clock. I literally walked in here on time."

"On time. On time? Mrs. Perfect always shows up early, so I did that, too," Robbie slurred. "I've been sitting here for an hour already, drinking alone."

Beck was feeling pretty grateful for the years of dealing with Robbie's entitled whining because she knew to plaster an empty smile on her face and ask, "So what do you want to talk to me about?" instead of breaking a beer bottle over his head.

"First, I think you should drink." Robbie gestured to the watered-down cranberry vodka in front of her.

"Why, did you rufie it?"

"No!" Robbie's pitch-dark eyes sparked with anger, and he ran his hand through his blond highlighted hair. Shelly must like him looking all vogue because Robbie was a pipe layer and had no use for hair appointments before he'd left her. "Look, you're always so uptight, and we always get into a battle, but I remember you were always a happy drunk."

"Always a happy drunk? The two times you drank with me, I was a happy drunk." She leaned forward and lowered her voice. "You know I was happy because you decided to take time off work and actually take me out, right?"

"God," Robbie drawled, tossing his head

back. "You know what your problem was?"

"I don't want to know."

"You were always so fucking needy." He pitched his voice high. "Cuddle me. Let's fuck while we stare at each other. You don't hold hands with me enough."

"*Ever*, Robbie. You didn't hold hands with me ever, and I told you I don't want to hear my shortfalls. We're divorced, so we really don't have to rehash this. Just please, tell me what you want."

Robbie crossed his arms over his chest and leaned back in the chair, then looked pointedly at her drink.

She let off a little growl and said, "Fine," then slurped it through the straw until it was gone.

"You look different," Robbie said as he lifted his hand at the passing waitress. "She'll have another," he told her. "A double."

"Hi, Layla," Beck greeted the pretty blonde.

"Publicist," Layla said, pointing her pen at her. "What do you actually want because I saw your face when you downed your drink. It wasn't your favorite."

"I'll have a long island ice tea, thanks."

"No, thank you," Layla said. "I heard what you're doing for us. I'm a fan of anyone rallying for us."

"For us?" Robbie said, his dark eyes narrowing to hate-filled slits at the bartender. "Are you one of those *shifters,* too?" He said the word like a curse, which was ridiculous because he'd been married to a shifter once and his son was also a shifter.

Beck wanted to throat-punch the judgmental asshole.

Layla plastered on a smile that didn't reach her eyes. "I am not a shifter."

"Good for you," Robbie slurred.

"But he is," Layla said, pointing to a tatted-up, dark-headed behemoth behind the bar. Kong narrowed his eyes at Robbie. Layla smoothed her apron over the swell of her belly, "And my baby will be, too." Her smile dipped to nothing. "Start shit in here, and I'll throw you out so fast you'll think I'm a fucking wizard." She turned to her mate and called out, "A long island for our mighty publicist and nothing more for this dick. He's cut off."

"Yeeep," Kong said as he spun a glass in his palm like a bartending pro. His angry eyes flashed an inhuman green at Robbie before Kong went back to work.

Mason broke a rack of balls over on the pool table where he was hanging out with

Haydan and Kellen of the Ashe Crew, who'd just walked in. The sound of balls scattering was deafening in the bar. It wasn't yet rush hour, and only a few of the tables were full. Even with his eyes flashing a furious, inhuman color, Mason looked sexy as hell lining up his next shot.

"Hellooo," Robbie said, snapping in front of her face.

With a slow, infuriated blink, she gave McFartFace her attention again.

"What I have to say will make you angry."

"Just say it," she muttered.

"Shelly and I are getting married."

Not shocking. They'd been together through half of Beck and Robbie's marriage. "Congratulations," she said in a dead voice.

"Because she's pregnant."

How romantic. "Double congratulations."

"With twins."

Beck prayed for patience, counted to three, then murmured, "Robbie, that's fine. I'm not angry. I'm glad for you that you're sticking with Shelly. I mean, you two have been together for a long time." She had tried not to sound bitter, but a little eked through. "And it'll be good for Ryder to have some half-siblings." She guessed. But on second thought, maybe this would hurt him if he saw his father being a good parent to his other kids. Huh. Now her chest was filling with dread. She hadn't been able to mold Robbie into good father material, but maybe Shelly had powers Beck didn't possess.

"The thing is…my other babies will be human."

Uh oh. Beck dragged her hands under the table and clenched them in her lap until her nails dug into her palms. "So?"

"So Shelly doesn't like that Ryder Changes into that hairy little bird whenever he wants. She don't like taking care of him."

"Well, she doesn't take care of him, so crisis averted."

"Yeah, but having him a month a year is going to be hard if she don't want him in our house."

"Robbie, you're his father—"

"And as his father I should have a say in his treatment."

"Treatment?"

Robbie pulled a stack of pamphlets from his pocket and slammed them on the table. The title of the first one shocked her into stillness. *Experimental Gene Treatment.*

Heat crept up her neck and into her

cheeks, then landed in her ears as she pulled the pamphlet open. The first paragraph alone made her sick to her stomach.

"They are trying to fix shifters."

"Fix. Shifters." Her voice shook like a leaf in a hurricane.

"Yeah, Beck, fix shifters because I'll be good goddamned if I watch you become all loud and proud, registering and shit, and shaming my name. My kid ain't meant to have a fucking owl in him." Robbie's voice filled with bone-chilling vitriol. "You tricked me. You never admitted you were a shifter. Not when we were dating, not when you got pregnant, not when we got married. I had a right to know what I was getting myself into."

"I didn't tell you because you're anti-shifter, Robbie!"

"Doesn't matter your reasons, Beck. I had to find out my kid was a freak when he turned into a fucking fuzzy baby owl right after his first birthday. That's messed up."

"Ryder's not a freak." She clenched her hands tighter until warmth trickled down her palms from where her nails dug in. She wanted to kill him. She wanted to Change and claw his eyes out for what he was suggesting. "Six months, Robbie. This pamphlet says the experiments will last half a damned year. You would torture the animal from our son, then? Is that what this is? You'd rather him be 'normal' than healthy? He is normal! I'm normal," she said, pressing her bleeding palms against her chest.

"No, you aren't, Beck. Your eyes are glowing like yellow highlighters right now. What are you going to do? Huh? You gonna homeschool him forever, keep him from making friends, coddle him because that's what you're doing. He ain't living! Every time he gets pissed, he Changes."

"Because you hurt him, Robbie! You hurt his feelings when you tell him he's not normal, or that he needs to change a fundamental part of who he is to earn your love. I'm not having this conversation anymore. My answer is a definite, non-negotiable no. Ryder is fine the way he is. He's perfect." Angry tears stung her eyes at how much she hated Robbie right now. She shook her head as she stared at this terrible person she'd given her heart to once. "Why can't you see he's perfect?"

"Because he ain't," Robbie gritted out. "And if you aren't willing to take him to the appointments on the days you have him, I'll file for primary custody and get it done myself."

"No judge is going to give you primary custody, you idiot. You barely see your son! You haven't paid child support! You are literally the worst father I've ever met."

"Yeah." Robbie gave her a blood-chilling smile. "But I'm human, and I have more rights than you do. A judge will see what I'm trying to do for him and cut you out of Ryder's life because he deserves better than this. He deserves better than you."

Bile rose in her throat at the idea that this monster could actually take Ryder away. Her son's life would be so empty, so lacking with Robbie constantly belittling him. She loved Ryder more than air. He was vital to her. Her entire existence was devoted to giving him a good life. She breathed for his little smile. "I'm leaving."

She stood, but Robbie grabbed her hand and growled out, "Not until you say yes and sign the consent forms."

Beck tried to break away from his grip, but Robbie tightened it, his eyes going cold as a snake's.

When he wrenched her closer, she gasped out, "You're hurting me."

The crash of the pool stick against the

metal edge of the pool table was deafening, and in an instant, the jagged splintered end was shoved against Robbie's jugular.

"Take your fuckin' hand off her," Mason gritted out in a low, snarling voice that could rival a monster's.

Robbie let her go slowly, then lifted his hands in surrender. Behind Mason, Haydan, Kellen, and Kong stood like demon-eyed titans, ready to rip Robbie in half.

"Here's how this will go," Mason said low as he eased the stick away from Robbie's throat. "There will be no more talk of torturing Beck's kid and no more laying your hands on her."

"And who are you?" Robbie asked through a furious grimace.

"I'm Mason. I'm Beck's mate." He gave a venomous smile under those glowing blue eyes. "Now, I've seen a lot of daddies like you."

"Like me," Robbie scoffed.

"Yeah. Fuck-up dickheads who screw up a kid's life because it suits your own to do it. And the story is always the same. You slither back into your kid's life when they're grown and don't need you anymore. You come with your apologies ready because your guilt will eat at you until you can't sleep. Can't eat. You'll raise your other two babies and eventually you will grow up enough to realize you did your other kid wrong. And you know what will happen then?"

Robbie crossed his arms defensively, but now he wouldn't meet Mason's glare.

The table creaked under Masons weight as he locked his arms on it and leaned forward. "He'll be the one telling you that you're worthless. And his hatred will be all your fault. You'll die knowing you failed that kid, when all he wanted was for you to care about him. Don't you bring this gene therapy shit up again. You won't kill Ryder's owl. He's a badass bird of prey. You'll just make him angry, and someday, he's going to be a fucking warrior, fed on your endless faults."

Mason arched his gaze to Beck, apparently waiting for her to chime in, but she was a little dumbfounded right about now. Before, it had always been her alone sticking up for Ryder, but Mason had just reminded her how awesome it was to be a shifter. Ryder *was* going to be a badass. He was a bird of prey, a raptor, a flight shifter. That was fucking awesome! She knew because she was one and, hell yeah, she was tough.

"I think you should leave," she murmured

to Robbie. "You should go back home and really get to know our son. He's amazing if you would just see past your prejudice."

Robbie shook his head for a long time, stared out the front window as the fire dimmed in his eyes. "Beck, I can't do this anymore."

"Can't do what?"

Robbie leveled her with a hard look and murmured, "That was my last offer to be a part of his life."

"I don't understand," Beck said softly.

"I don't want to pay no child support on a kid I never wanted."

Mason gave her a sad look and moved off with the others, leaving her and Robbie alone again.

"Robbie, you don't pay child support now, and I still let you see him whenever you want."

"Yeah, but we already went through the courts, and last paycheck, they docked me by a lot. I have two kids on the way, Shelly can't stand shifters, and she needs more than you did, Beck. She needs the big house and the shiny new car to be happy."

"So what do you want me to do? I can't afford to go back to court to beg them to stop docking your pay, and even if I did, that stuff isn't up to me. And frankly, you should've been paying something. He is your son too, and you've put the entire financial burden of raising our child on me."

"I think I want that burden to stay on you."

She shook her head in confusion, unable to come up with a single response.

"I think I want to give up my parental rights."

Beck huffed out a shocked sound. "W-what?"

"Your man or mate or whatever is right. I'm one-hundred percent going to screw Ryder up. I don't like shifters, Beck. Never have. I don't think you're natural. You don't fit into the food chain."

"We fit fine. You just hate that I'm higher on the food chain than you," she gritted out.

"I still want the gene therapy. If it was up to me, I'd strip that owl out of Ryder tomorrow and be done with it. I'm not putting my new family's needs second by giving you all my money to raise a *shifter*. If you're going to fight fixing Ryder, then I'm out."

And with that, Robbie stood and left without looking back.

SEVENTEEN

"Okay, thanks June. And no matter what happens, you guys will still be in his life. You've been amazing grandparents."

"Well, I sure appreciate that," June said in a tear-soaked voice. "I just wish Robbie wasn't so bone-headed. Call us tomorrow and let us know if we need to meet you halfway."

"Okay. Have a good night."

"You too, honey. Bye."

Beck hung up the phone and set it in her lap, face up in case Robbie called to change his mind. Although, according to his mom, June, relenting his rights had been on his mind for a while now.

"I should've seen this coming," Beck said softly to Mason from the passenger's seat. "Ryder's already asleep so I couldn't talk to him. God, I hope Robbie is in his right mind when he talks to him about this. Or should he even say anything? I mean, Ryder might not realize Robbie isn't in his life anymore because he really wasn't present to begin with. I don't know what the right thing is to do. I don't know anything," she whispered helplessly.

Mason intertwined his fingers with hers and lifted her knuckles to his lips. "Everything is going to be okay."

"Will it? Genetic testing! I still can't even wrap my head around that. Robbie's ultimatum was to physically and emotionally scar Ryder or reject his child altogether? I already felt alone raising Ryder, but now I'm really, really alone."

"No you aren't," Mason said fiercely. He looked at her with the fire of promise in his eyes. "We'll figure this all out."

But Mason didn't see what she did. His headlights illuminated a woman in the middle of the road. She was cast in an eerie blue glow, her long dark hair flowing unnaturally, and her eyes were black as night.

"Mason!" Beck screamed. "Look out!"

Mason jerked his attention to the road and slammed on the brakes, skidding sideways right into the woman. But right before they careened into her, she disappeared.

A terrifying whisper filled the cab. "They're coming."

"Hold on!" Mason demanded, turning into the skid with one hand pressing Beck so hard against the seat she couldn't breathe.

Fishtail after fishtail spun the truck this way and that, and the smell of burnt rubber choked Beck as they slammed to a final stop.

"Oh shit, oh shit, oh shit," Beck chanted, horrified as her heart threatened to leap out of her chest. She turned and looked behind them, expecting to see a body on the road, even though there had been no impact. "What was that?"

"That," Mason gritted out, his furious gaze on the rearview mirror, "was Esmerelda."

****

Mason ran his finger under the covers, along her ribs, and down the curve of her stomach to the swell of her hips. "Can't sleep?"

"Sorry," Beck whispered in the dark. "I was trying to be still so you could get some rest."

He brushed her hair out of the way and pressed his lips on the back of her neck. "I can't sleep either."

Easing back against his strength, she whispered, "Why does it feel like everything is falling down around us? Our rights are being stripped, Robbie...Esmerelda. I've been thinking about it a lot, and I think I understand about the claiming mark now."

Mason sighed and hooked his arm around her stomach, pulled her tight to him. "Beck, it's not that I don't think about it. I mean, I feel obsessed. My boar wants you, I want you, and damn, I will love seeing my mark on you someday."

"But Esmerelda. She's getting stronger in your life, just like I am, and you want to know why before you give me a mark. You don't want it to be me and Esmerelda fighting for your attention when you claim me. You want it to be about me and no one else."

"Close. I want it to be about you and Ryder. He's my only shot at a kid, Beck. I feel like you've opened this door to a life I thought I would never have."

"Do you feel pressure?"

"Yeah. Hell, yeah. Before Esmerelda, I would've jumped right on you, marked you, claimed you. I was young, but Beck, I was so ready for a family. A mate, kids, all of it. I was right on the cusp of taking the alpha position over my people. I had a great job. Providing for you and Ryder wouldn't have been a concern at all, and back then, that was the most important thing to me. Security."

"I'm not asking you to provide for us, Mason."

"No, that's not what I'm saying. I have the means to provide for you now, too, but when I met you, that wasn't the first thing I thought about. I'm different now. The first thing I thought was, 'oh shit, how can I make her happy while I'm dragging this baggage?' And the answer is I don't know if I can. I couldn't make Esmerelda happy, and now look what's happened. She wasted her last years on me, and now she's wasting her afterlife on me, too."

Beck turned in his arms. Her night vision was impeccable so she could see every worried line of his face, every indentation of muscle across his shoulders, every ounce of sorrow in his dark gaze. "I don't think she would see it as a waste."

Mason traced the outside of her ear with a light touch. "Jason said he thinks she's here to tell me to pay attention to you and Ryder. He thinks she's here to tell me to move on from her death."

Beck searched his eyes, but he wasn't meeting her gaze anymore. "And what do you think?"

"I was fine with that explanation until I saw her standing in that road tonight. I'm letting you in. I'm falling in love with you. I'm nervous, but excited to meet Ryder." Mason lifted his soft brown eyes to hers, held her steady there. "So why is Esmerelda getting stronger?"

Beck shook her head helplessly. "I don't know." That had scared her badly. She'd already been freaked out by Esmerelda talking to her in the restaurant, but seeing her and feeling her cold, dead breath against her neck in Mason's truck had stolen the safety Beck felt here. Sure, she'd known ghosts existed, but physically seeing a ghost, feeling Esmerelda's presence, and watching the effect it had on her mate was completely different. Her owl hadn't settled down since they'd almost wrecked. *Scratch, scratch, scratch,* her inner bird of prey clawed at her skin, asking to be released just so she could fly off some of this emotion.

"Will you Change with me?" she whispered, too chicken to look him directly in the face and watch the rejection there.

Mason hooked a finger under her chin and lifted her face, pressed his lips to hers. His mouth moved against hers like water, soft and gentle. And when his tongue brushed hers, she opened for him, allowing him to taste her, allowing him in. Although she wouldn't admit it out loud, Mason had all of her. Everything she had to offer, he could have if he would just keep her. Because this feeling—this chest fluttering, stomach-dipping, happy sensation—hadn't existed before he'd breathed life into her.

He was afraid he wouldn't be able to make her happy because he felt broken. But he didn't see it. She was broken, too, shattered into the perfect shape to match his tattered edges. He could keep his claiming mark and take it slow if that's what he needed. She understood now, and she would wait for him. She would find her patience if it meant she could live more moments like this when a big, dominant, scarred-up beast of a man held her heart so gently in his hand and promised wordlessly to protect it for always.

She loved him. *Loved* him. Just being capable of this intense emotion after Robbie had stripped her soul bare was a testament to how inherently good Mason was. She wouldn't have given herself to anyone less. Not after all she'd been through.

So she would wait. And she would love him. And she wouldn't guilt him for being careful because he'd nurtured deep love once, and even if he didn't realize it yet, Mason *knew* how to build it again. With her.

He was worth waiting for. Worth the effort. Worthy of her "all in."

With a content sigh, she slipped out of his kiss with a soft smack and rolled over, gave him her back. Her revved-up instincts told her Mason really was a beast boar. Robbie used to take her from behind and hurt her, and she'd sworn never to let a man do that to her again. But then Mason had come along, and he wasn't just some human male trying to dominate her. Trying to stifle her shifter by putting her beneath him. Sex with Mason was different. It was more animalistic, and this was the test. If he didn't trigger her to panic, then she really was getting better.

Mason's reaction was instant. His arms slid around her, pulled her back tight against his raging hard erection. He rolled his hips gracefully with her seductive movement. And when she reached behind her and gripped the back of his neck, she could feel his teeth on her shoulder, as if he couldn't help but tempt himself to bite.

She thought he would take her hard and fast since that's what rutting men did, but instead, Mason slid his hand down her quivering belly and cupped her sex. And when he brushed his finger down her wet folds, she gasped and spread her knees wider for him. For a while, he toyed gently with her clit, bringing her closer to climax with every touch, and when she was bowing against him, pleading, he finally slipped his finger inside of her.

Against her back, Mason rolled his long, thick erection. She wanted that. Wanted him in her, wanted them connected, because when they were in each other's arms, the rest of the world slipped away. Beck reached between her legs and drew his dick between her thighs, against his hand as he fingered her.

Mason grunted and pushed a second finger inside of her, and she was gone. Her orgasm pulsed through her, and he worked each aftershock out of her until she was sensitive and twitching under his touch. And then he kissed her neck as she recovered. Sensual, commanding lips, a hint of tongue, and nipping teeth had her begging silently again. She arched back, tempting him as his dick slid through her wet heat.

"Are you sure," he whispered against her neck.

Oh, he'd listened when she'd told him Robbie used to take her from behind just so he didn't have to look at her face, but this was different. Mason was different. Sex like this with her mate was exciting and erotic. She loved that he made her come before he took pleasure for himself. Good man. Good boar. Good mate.

"With you, I'm sure."

Mason rolled her up on her hands and knees and threw the covers off them. "On your elbows," he said in a gravelly voice. "Arch that back for me so I don't hurt you."

A delicious shiver trembled up her spine and landed in her shoulders at the commanding confidence in his voice. She bowed like a stretching feline and spread her knees farther apart on the soft mattress. "Like this?" she teased, tossing him a look over her shoulder.

Mason's eyes sparked like blue fire, his gaze locked between her legs.

He ran his big, calloused hands down the sensitive skin of her outer thighs, lifted up on his knees, and pressed his taut stomach against her back, like he was testing how much weight she could bear. Rocking them forward gently, he brushed her sex with the head of his cock, and now he was the one teasing.

"Touch yourself," he whispered, hand over hers, guiding it between her legs.

Touch herself? Eeek! She hadn't ever done that in front of anyone before, and now—oooooh. Mason pressed her hand over her clit, and she could feel his shaft as he dipped into her by inches. He eased back and then pushed into her deeper, filling her with delicious pressure, stretching her with his girth.

His arm was locked on the bed beside her cheek, and she turned and bit his bicep as he rubbed her hand between her legs again. A low rumble rattled his chest, vibrating against her back.

"Deeper," she pleaded.

Mason pushed into her until his hips met her ass. Rolling her eyes closed, Beck sighed out a helpless sound as she moved with him. His abs flexed against her as he pulled out and pushed in, and when she pressed his hand against her sex to feel where he was entering her, to feel how wet he'd made her, Mason jerked his hips, bucking into her faster.

She was already toeing the edge, about to fall over the side when Mason slammed into her with one more deep thrust, and... "I'm coming," she gasped out. "Mason, I'm coming."

Mason bucked into her again and froze, gritting out a feral sound as his dick pulsed heat inside of her. Over and over he throbbed, matching her release, until warmth trickled down her thighs. God, she loved this. Loved him wild. Loved how he made her feel like the sexiest woman on the planet. Her sexy beast boar, filling her with his seed until she couldn't hold anymore.

Minutes stretched on as they slowed their pace and savored every aftershock, and at last, with a slick sound, Mason pulled out of her.

He ran kisses down her back, right along her spine, coveting her, showing her sex wasn't his end game. Showing her it was just the beginning of his affection. "Yes," he whispered against her fevered skin.

"Yes, what?" she asked in the dark.

"Yes, I would love to Change with you."

The grin that stretched her face felt so good. Wordlessly, Mason stood beside the bed and held out his hand, palm up.

"I should clean up," she murmured, slipping her hand into his.

Mason lifted his chin proudly, his blue eyes glowing from the inside out. "No. My animal likes you smelling like me."

With a steadying breath, she padded out of

the bedroom, through the living room, and into the night, holding the hand of the man she loved. Mason didn't mind touching her anymore. He didn't balk or panic. In fact, the sound rattling his chest, just above her senses, sounded content, and his skin heated where it touched hers. She couldn't even bring herself to be embarrassed by the warm wetness that trickled down the insides of her thighs to her knees. If this was the only mark Mason would allow himself on her, then she was fine with smelling like him.

"You first," he said low. "I like to watch you take off."

Beck's heart fluttered like wings in her chest. Whether that was from the giddy feeling he gave her or from her owl proudly testing her wings inside, she didn't know. Lifting up on the balls of her bare feet, she kissed him, brushed her tongue against his once, then stood back, proud of her animal for the first time in her life. Why? Because Mason loved her, not despite her animal, but partly because of her animal. There was beauty in that—in being accepted completely, owl and all.

With a quick breath to brace for the instant pain that always came with her Change, Beck hunched inward and let her animal explode from her skin. She could see everything in this form. Every facet of Mason's beautiful, awed face. Every rippling muscle on his body as he strode forward on his powerful legs and lifted his face to watch her circle above him. The trailer park below her was silent in the hours before dawn, but his slow smile was like music. It filled her head with joy. Filled her with the idea that despite the scar he withheld, she was really his. The proud look on his face said as much.

She let off a long screech, inviting his boar to come out and play. She'd never shifted with anyone, and how fitting that Mason was her first. The white of Mason's breathtaking smile flashed in the instant before his beastly boar ripped from his skin. His coarse, black hair spiked up in a line down his back, and his tusks shone white against the dark. His eyes were the blue inhuman color she'd come to adore instead of fear. She waited to feel afraid as flight shifters often did around shifters higher on the food chain, but all she felt was an overwhelming elation that he was hers. Her safety, her mate, her love. Whooo whooo was the lucky owl? Beck was.

She circled around as Mason trotted for the tree line on those sure, glossy black hooves of his. Dive-bombing closer, she cried out a happy noise as Mason lifted his head, cutting proudly through the air with his razor sharp tusks. Nothing could hurt her with a mate like him. Big barrel chest, powerful front legs, head high, ears erect, tusks ready for ripping, muscles moving easily with every galloping step. Mason was grace and power. He was perfection. *Mine*, her possessive owl declared.

Together they wound through the Boarlander woods, faster and faster, ducking and dodging the ancient pines of the forest. Mason wove through trails just below her, while she zigzagged gracefully around the trunks, her eyes ever dancing back to him. With a grunt, Mason looked up at her, then pushed his legs faster. Damn, he was quick, and she heaved breath as she rushed to keep up with him. God, she loved this—the wind brushing through her flight feathers, the night sounds quieting as they passed, the noise of Mason's breath below her. Steam puffed in front of his face in the cool night air as he ran faster. She'd never felt joy like this. She'd never felt complete freedom. Changes near her hometown had to be done carefully so that no one saw a snowy owl where one didn't belong. Here, in Damon's mountains, she was safe to be herself. Safe to fly fast and far, and her mate was below, pushing her to test her wings.

When they came to a clearing, Mason skidded to a stop, billowing dust around him while Beck spread her wings against the breeze and thrust her talons out to assist in her quick slow-down. Beneath her, the fireflies had kicked up in the meadow. Little blinking dots lit up the night, like stars come to earth. Mesmerized, she circled lower and landed gently on the muscular hump between Mason's shoulder blades. If her talons digging into his tough hide for balance bothered him, he didn't show it. Instead, Mason relaxed under her and looked over his shoulder, his eyes soft and contrasting starkly against the ferocity of his warrior face.

And when he gave his attention back to the sparkling meadow, she flapped her wings languidly for balance. One of her downy white feathers floated down onto Mason's dark bristled fur. How different they were on the outside, but how similar they were on the inside.

The fireflies lifted higher and higher, spreading out into the woods and reminding her that magic moments like this existed to brighten dark days. She'd been overwhelmed by the grit only a few hours ago, and then Mason had soothed her and gifted her beautiful relief.

Mason had been wrong when he'd questioned if he could make her happy.

Because here, in the firefly meadow, clinging to the strong back of the boar she loved, Beck had never been happier.

EIGHTEEN

Mason cracked his knuckles and paced in front of 1010 again. Maybe he wouldn't be so nervous about meeting Ryder if Beck didn't look sick to her stomach with worry.

Robbie would be here any minute with Beck's five-year-old boy, and so much was riding on this. Flight shifters were notoriously fierce parents, and Beck held information about Ryder close to her chest. Drawing details from her lips about her son was like pulling teeth, and when he'd asked Beck, "Why?" she'd told him, "I guess I've always had to hide him away to protect him, so I learned to keep him to myself."

Made sense. She'd been raising Ryder in the human world, distant from any shifters, and with a human mate who didn't accept the animals in either her or Ryder.

Beck's body rang with tension as she stood near the entrance of the Boarland Mobile Park, talking into the phone too low for Mason to hear all the way from back here. Likely, she was directing Robbie where to go. God, what was taking him so long? Anyone with eyes in their head could see Beck needed to see her son, and now each minute was dragging.

The other Boarlanders were down in Saratoga, participating in a charity bake sale Beck had set up for them. It was at the community center, and she was supposed to be making a pro-shifter speech in a few hours, but she'd been right when she had told him everything worked on Robbie's schedule. He was already two hours later than what they'd planned.

Beck stood on tiptoes, watching the road, and Mason could hear it now—the soft rumble of a truck engine kicking up gravel in the distance.

He was going to be sick. This was his shot at a family, but if Ryder didn't take to him, he had no doubt in his mind Beck would tuck her little owl under one arm and sacrifice her happiness for her son's.

Shit. He should've read some of those parenting books Beaston had. Now he was panicking, feeling like Ryder would hate him for sure, Beck would leave, and the cracks in his soul that Esmerelda had left would be blasted wide open.

Breathe.

Mason forced himself to sit on the bottom stair of 1010's porch because every instinct urged him to rush to Beck's side and rub her shoulders and promise her everything would be okay. This wasn't about him, though. It was her hurt and Ryder's pain, and his sole responsibility in this matter would be to listen and be there for them as they picked their way through this.

An old, rust-eaten, navy Chevy bounced and bumped under the Boarland Mobile Park sign, then smoothed out as Robbie hit the newly paved part of the road. Through the window, Robbie gave Beck a hate-filled glare as she waved back in response to the little hand waving out the window.

"Robbie, stop!" she cried as he coasted past her.

"Momma!" Ryder yelled through the open window, reaching for her.

Goddamn, Mason hated Robbie. Clenching his hands, Mason stood as the asshole made his way in a straight line toward 1010, forcing

Beck to jog after his truck.

Robbie skidded to a stop right in the newly sodded yard and shoved the door open with a *creeeaak*. He barreled toward Mason, but halted when Mason stood to his full height and gave him a don't-you-fuckin'-dare glare.

"I just want to see my kid's new dad in the light. It's your fault, right?"

Behind Robbie, Beck was pulling a little golden-haired boy from the front seat and hugging him tight against her chest.

"Man, I don't want this. I don't want you cutting out on your kid's life," Mason said low.

"Yeah, well I did some thinkin'. And Beck used to be a pushover. She was. She let me have girlfriends for years before she asked for that divorce. If I said 'jump,' she said 'how high,' but now suddenly she can't get on board with doing something that will give her son a good life?"

"By *stripping* the animal out of him?" Mason gritted out, about to lose his shit on this motherfucker's face. "There isn't anything wrong with him. Nothing. You, on the other hand…you're all kinds of messed up for even considering torture as an option."

Robbie huffed a humorless breath, his dark eyes sparking with fury. After running his hands through his highlighted, stupid-looking hair, he looked like a pissed-off porcupine. Mason could squash him with a look if he wanted.

"I want to see the shit-hole you'll be raising my son in."

"What?" Mason asked as the idiot shoved past him and up the stairs. "We haven't even discussed that stuff, and this isn't my trailer."

Robbie stomped across the new porch in heavy soled work boots, but yelped when his leg went straight through a floorboard. He let off a string of muttered curses. The dangling *0* of the house number that had been holding on by a single rusty nail for so long suddenly loosed and fell onto Robbie's head with a resonating *cong*. An accidental laugh huffed from Mason's chest. 1010 was fighting back.

"What the fuck?" Robbie shouted, struggling to free his lanky leg from the splintered jaws of the porch where he'd sunk hip-deep.

"Ten-ten apparently doesn't like being called a shit-hole. You just got your ass kicked by a thirty-five-year-old trailer, mister. Might want to leave now before it eats you whole."

Robbie struggled out of the broken porch like a beached trout, then stood in a huff and rubbed his head. "It's your fault Beck is being such a pain in the ass about all this."

"Okay." Mason bit his tongue against the verbal lashing he wanted to give this entitled little shit because that wouldn't help Beck or Ryder.

"I don't like him," Robbie yelled, jamming his finger at Mason.

Beck approached the porch, Ryder clinging to her tightly, and tears had already rimmed her eyes. "You don't have to like him. Who I pick has nothing to do with you, just like I couldn't say anything about who you picked."

"Well..." Robbie hooked his hands on his hips. "I think it's messed up that you came here to work, and instead you moved on inappropriately fast from what we had."

Mason pursed his lips and convinced himself not to whack this moron upside the head. Robbie had started banging Shelly way before he and Beck were even separated, so the fact that he thought he had any right to judge her was downright laughable.

Beck sighed and looked exhausted. "Can we talk about this in private, away from Ryder?"

"Nah, our little freak should hear what a whore his mom—*gulp*."

Mason tightened his hand around Robbie's throat and narrowed his eyes at the little cretin. "I could pop your face off your body with little effort, and you calling Beck a whore in front of her kid is making that prospect mighty tempting. Best go carry this conversation on in private, and mind the names you call her, yeah?"

Robbie made choking sounds and scratched at Mason's fingers, trying to loosen his grip. "Okay," he rasped out.

Mason gave him an empty smile and dropped Robbie back to earth.

Beck stood there wide-eyed, legs splayed, holding Ryder's face against her neck. Slowly, she lowered her son to the ground and knelt in front of him. "Ryder, this is Mason. He's our friend. Would you mind hanging out with him for a few minutes while I talk to Daddy?"

The little boy's lip was pouted out, and his eyes, the same seafoam green of his mother's, were filling with tears. In a broken whisper, the boy said, "That's not my dad. He said don't call him that no more."

Fuckin' Robbie.

Beck looked gutted and kissed each of her son's palms, then patted him on the bottom and watched as he climbed the stairs slowly.

When he got to Mason, Ryder arched his neck way back. He looked scared. Mason had that effect on people.

Beck's gaze lingered on her son as she followed Robbie to the tree line. Geez, Mason wished he could be there, but Beck was strong and had been taking what Robbie dished out for a long time. She could handle herself, and besides...she'd asked him to stay with her son.

Clearing his throat, Mason squatted down to eye-level and said, "What your dad called you..."

"F-freak," Ryder whispered.

Mason leveled him with a look and gripped his tiny shoulders. And with a slow smile, he said, "You're not." Pointing to the first trailer on the left, he said, "You know what kind of shifters live there?"

Ryder's eyes went round. "They have animals, too?"

Mason nodded. "A great grizzly bear and a white tiger." He pointed to each trailer as he said, "Silverback gorilla, bear, bear," and when he pointed to the trailer behind him, he grinned even bigger and said, "You know who lives here?"

"Who?"

Mason chuckled at his little owl *hoo*. "The

coolest shifter of all. Your mom. The awesome, fast-flying, sharp-clawed bird of prey, snowy owl."

"Like me," Ryder said, the corner of his lips trembling into a smile before it disappeared again.

Mason nodded and pointed to his frail chest. "Just like you."

"Are you a monster, too?"

"Nah, there's no monsters here, Ryder. We're all normal, just like you. You want to guess what kind of animal I have?"

Ryder nodded solemnly. "A bear?"

"Nope."

"One of Santa's reindeer?"

Mason laughed and shook his head. "Nope."

"What are you?"

"I'm a boar shifter."

"What's a boar?"

"It's a big, giant…pig."

A fit of tinkling giggles shook Ryder's little shoulders, and the tightness that had been constricting Mason's chest loosened at the sound of the boy's laughter. He would be okay. Mason would make sure of it.

Robbie's yelling reached them on the breeze, and Ryder twisted around, looked scared again, and the next time Mason got a peek at his eyes, they were bright yellow.

"You want to Change?" he asked easily.

"I'm not supposed to."

"You can Change whenever you want to here. Your mom just Changed last night and flew all around the woods."

"I cain't fly yet," he said in that squeaky voice with the little country accent that was making Mason want to cuddle him up and erase all the damage Robbie had done.

"Ah, but someday you will."

"All I do is get mad and turn into a little bird and just sit there."

"Well, that's what little birds do. You'll get your flight feathers when you grow up big and strong, and then you can fly all around with your mom."

Ryder looked off in the direction of Robbie's yelling, then back at Mason. His eyes were blazing the color of the sun. "I don't like when he yells at me and Momma. If I Change, you won't get mad and tell on me?"

"Never. I Change a lot, too."

"Into a pig?"

Mason grinned. "Yep. Change if you want, and I'll sit right here and keep you safe, okay?"

Ryder's little voice dropped to a whisper.

"Promise?"

Mason swallowed hard a couple of times. He would bet broken promises to this kid numbered in the hundreds. That wasn't him, though, and from here on, Mason was going to show him that a man could follow-through and keep his word. "Always."

And then with a little squeak of pain, Ryder disappeared under his clothes.

Carefully, Mason plucked his green T-shirt away, and his heart froze in his chest as he laid eyes on the tiny, fluffy, gray and white owlet.

Mine.

Choked up on emotion, Mason asked, "Do you want to sit with me?"

Ryder swayed on his feet a few clumsy steps toward Mason, his little curved talons clicking on the wooden board beneath him. He looked up at Mason with those yellow trusting eyes, so much like Beck's when her animal was close to the surface. He blinked slowly, one eye quicker than the other.

My boy.

As gentle as he could, Mason cupped his hands around Ryder, then rested his back against the side of 1010. And slowly, so he wouldn't harm one perfect, downy feather on Ryder's frail body, he cupped the owlet to his chest and let off a trembling breath as he blinked back the burning sensation in his eyes.

My little bird.

When he looked toward the tree line, Robbie's neck was red and veiny from yelling. Mason locked eyes with Beck, whose face was transforming into the most beautiful smile, like her ex and all his poisonous words had melted away and all she saw was him and Ryder.

Mason returned her smile as a warm, tingling sensation unfurled in his chest.

My family.

NINETEEN

"Mason," Ryder whispered.

Beck cracked her sleepy eyes open in time to see Mason's shoulder shake under her son's little hand. She gave a private smile and stretched.

"Mason," Ryder said louder.

"Mmmm," Mason rumbled. "What is it, boy?"

"I'm hungry." A smile tinged Ryder's tone. "I want bacon."

Beck stifled a sleepy laugh. This had been the game for a week straight.

"No bacon in this house, boy."

Readying for tickles, Ryder hunched in on himself, grinning big in his red flannel pajamas. To her son's giggling delight, Mason snaked his arm out and pulled Ryder close. Mason tickled him and then released the little early bird, who went scampering into the next room, trailing laughter behind him.

Beck's face hurt from smiling so wide. Fluffing up the pillow under her cheek, she watched Mason sit up in bed and run his hand sleepily through his hair, spiking it up in all directions. The shiny scar of her claiming mark contrasted with his smooth skin.

"You know you don't have to get up with him every morning," she murmured. "I'm more used to it than you."

Mason snorted. "Bull. I'm a logger. I'm no stranger to early mornings. Besides…I read women biologically require more sleep than men."

She believed him. When she'd sat down at the computer yesterday to answer emails, there had been a tab open. Mason had been searching the Internet for *how to make a woman happy*. And *let her sleep in* was number five on the page he'd pulled up.

She giggled and squeezed his hand as he stood. Mason gave her one of those sexy sleepy smiles as he pulled a pair of low-riding gray sweatpants over his briefs. No shirt for him, and it wasn't lost on her that Ryder had begun to ask to sleep without a shirt at night, too. He watched everything Mason did.

Watching them together over the past week had broken her heart wide open. After she got up and readied for the day, she knew what she would find when she padded into the kitchen. The first streaks of gray dawn were filtering through the small window over the kitchen sink, and in the dim light, her boys stood side by side in front of the stove. One stood so tall and strong, his head almost touched the low ceiling, and one, her little mini-me, stood on a red stepstool Mason had picked up at the store.

Her heart caught in her throat like it did every day that began like this. Silently, she rested her shoulder against the fridge and listened to them.

"Don't get too close to the hot coil now, boy. You'll singe your feathers, and your mom will have my hide."

"What's a hide?"

Mason poked Ryder's bony arm. "A hide means skin."

"Pigs have thick skins. Momma told me so."

As Mason stirred the eggs he was scrambling in the pan, he chuckled that deep sound that said he really enjoyed being around Ryder.

"Well, your mom's a wise woman, and she's right. When I'm Changed, it's hard to hurt me."

"I wish I was a pig shifter."

"Nah, boy. You'll see the value in your owl the older you get. I wish I could fly like you will someday. You want to fly like your mom, don't you?"

"But won't I be scared so high up?"

"Maybe the first time. It's okay to be scared, as long as you don't let it take you over."

"Can I crack an egg?"

"You think you're ready?"

Ryder arched his head way back to look at Mason and nodded once. "I'm ready."

"Do it in the bowl then."

Ryder smashed it into the bowl, and Mason laughed. "Pick out the shells."

"With my fingers? Grandma Junebug says I shouldn't touch eggs."

"Well, don't touch them at Grandma Junebug's house, but here you can touch them as long as you wash your hands after."

Ryder peeled into giggles as he picked through the slippery egg to chase shell fragments.

"Use those little talons, boy," Mason

teased.

"Hoo hoo," Ryder said in a barely audible voice as he dug harder.

Mason let out a loud, booming laugh.

God, it felt so good to hear Ryder talking openly about his animal. It hadn't ever been like that for him before and, apparently, he needed this acceptance, because ever since he'd come to the Boarland Mobile Park, he'd asked so many questions about his shifter side. Her little boy had garnered the fealty of every one of the Boarlanders in a matter of hours, and what an incredible experience for Beck to watch him fit in here. To watch the wariness in his eyes fade away. To watch him smile so often.

He hadn't asked about Robbie much, but when Beck had watched Mason tuck him in bed last night, she'd overheard Ryder tell him, "My dad doesn't like me." Mason had gone quiet for a minute as he tucked the comforter in all around him. Then he'd sighed and told him, "Your dad cares about you. He just doesn't know how to show it. But you know what? I like you." Ryder had nodded his little head and rolled over and hugged his favorite blanket tight. And just before Mason left the little guest room they'd set up for him, Ryder had murmured, "I like you, too."

And then Beck had gone outside and bawled her eyes out in the woods because her heart had been so touched by that tender moment. When she'd claimed Mason, she'd thought she couldn't love him more than in that moment. But then he'd been patient and tender with her, and she thought she couldn't love him anymore than in *that* moment. And then she'd seen him with Ryder…and she fell in love with him all over again, every day.

As they sat down for breakfast, chattering away about plans for the day, there was a commotion outside, and Clinton yelled out, "Mason! Beck!"

"What the hell?" Mason muttered.

"What the hell?" Ryder repeated, sliding off his chair.

"Don't say 'hell,'" Mason and Beck both said at the same time.

Mason made it to the door first and muttered a curse at whatever he saw outside. Beck was mighty tempted to repeat said curse the second she saw the patrol car flashing its lights right in the middle of Boarland Mobile Park. The Boarlanders were gathered around a pair of uniformed police officers, and from the looks of it, Ally was giving them hell.

"But it's against the law to register under crews now," Ally gritted out, her face a mask of fury as she held a stack of papers folded in her hand. Her short, platinum blond hair was mussed from sleep, and in the morning light her tattoos down her arm were stark against her pale skin.

"Right, so they'll be registered as lone shifters under no crew," the taller police officer explained as Beck and Mason approached.

"What's wrong, Momma?" Ryder asked, slipping his little hand into hers.

"I don't know, baby." He was small for his age and fine-boned like all bird shifters were, so she swung him up onto her hip and hugged him close.

"What's going on?" Mason asked.

"I'm Officer Dunlap, and this is my partner, Officer Moore," the shorter police officer said. He gestured to Beck. "We got a call from your ex-husband. He outed you as a non-registered shifter, along with your son and your mate. The registration process has begun based on the information he gave the Saratoga police department, but you'll have to fill out the rest of the paperwork, and the three of you will be fined for disobeying shifter registration laws."

Beck felt like she'd been slapped. Mason scanned the paperwork. "Mason Croy, Boar shifter," he read aloud. Eyes blazing, he glared at the officer. "I'll be the only registered boar shifter in the world. You'll put a huge target on my back. I didn't register for a reason." His horror-filled gaze drifted to Beck and Ryder. "Please. I'll pay the fines, do whatever you want me to do, but let me keep my animal off the record."

"I'm sorry. We didn't make the laws. We're just supposed to enforce them."

Ally huffed a furious breath. "I used to say that to justify what I was doing to innocent people. This is so messed up. How would you feel if you had to register your names in some screwed-up database? Your wife's name, your children's names. Huh?" Her voice pitched higher. "We've done what the government has asked—"

"They haven't," Dunlap said, pointing to Mason and Beck.

"Because they couldn't!"

"Please," Beck begged. "If I register, can you please give Mason and my son a pass? I'm asking you as a worried mother. As a worried mate. My ex is trying to get back at me for…I don't know. It shouldn't affect them, though."

"You three remaining unregistered is against the law." Dunlap's eyes pooled with regret, but he still handed Mason a new stack of paperwork. "Your total fines are three thousand four-hundred-thirty dollars. You can pay them at the courthouse in Saratoga when you fill in the blanks on your paperwork. You have forty-eight hours."

As the patrol car pulled a U-turn and drove out of Boarland Mobile Park, Mason scrubbed a hand down the three-day scruff on his jaw, then hugged Beck and Ryder up tight as he watched them disappear under the welcome sign.

The crew looked gutted. Harrison chucked a brick that had been sitting in the road as hard as he could into the trees and yelled a loud, resounding, "Shit!"

"I would *not* share pizza rolls with them," Bash said as he rubbed Emerson's belly gingerly. For the first time since Mason had come back to the Boarlanders, Bash wore a frown on his face instead of a smile.

"I need to Change," Kirk muttered, his eyes blazing gold.

"Me, too," Clinton said quietly as he followed the giant silverback shifter toward the tree line behind the trailers.

The others murmured their regret as they drifted off one by one, but Beck couldn't move. Couldn't move, couldn't breathe, couldn't think straight. The world would know she and Ryder were snowy owls now, some of the last of their kind. The world would know about Mason and assume he was the last of the boars since none of the others had registered. She'd felt safe for the first time in her life up in these mountains, and now Robbie had stripped that away from her.

Beck blinked hard and looked down at Ryder's sweet, frightened face. "It's okay," she murmured. God, she wished she could believe what she'd said, but when she looked up into Mason's somber eyes, something deep inside of her said that nothing was okay.

Before, Ryder had a right to marry who he wanted when he grew up. He could've chosen a mate and avoided the bullshit laws that were forced upon shifters, but now, he was just as affected as the rest. He was on the list. He was a target.

Mason pressed his lips to her forehead, but his attention was still on the woods where the cop car had disappeared. They weren't there yet, but now she and Mason could never legally wed. They couldn't even register to the same crew. Claiming a human mate was illegal, but what about the mark she'd left on him? Was that punishable by jail time like it was with humans?

Their only chance at being anything more than they were right now, in this moment, depended solely on humans voting to reinstate their rights.

Beck wasn't just building public relations for the shifters of Damon's mountains anymore.

Now she was fighting for her son, and her mate.

TWENTY

The papers in Beck's shaking hands made a pathetic shuffling noise. To escape the sound of her weakness, she inhaled deeply, held the air in her lungs for a three-count, then hugged the paperwork to her chest.

Beside her, Mason swung Ryder up on his shoulders, held his legs in place with one arm and pulled her against his side with the other. "I know you're worried."

"Mason, I just signed my kid's rights away. I just signed mine away." The morning sun peeked over the top of the courthouse. "Up until now, the shifter stuff worried me, but it didn't affect me. I was good at hiding. I was good at keeping us protected, and now I feel completely naked."

"You ain't naked, Momma," Ryder said from way up high on Mason's shoulders. "You got lots of clothes on."

Beck looked down at her power pants and matching charcoal-gray jacket. She smiled at Ryder. "It was just a metaphor. I meant vulnerable."

Ryder scrunched up his nose. "Huh. I'm hungry."

The worry didn't leave Mason's eyes, but he pulled her to a stop and squared up to her. "Beck, I swear I won't let anything happen to you and Ryder. You're mine to protect now. You aren't alone."

Her eyes burned with those damn traitorous tears that she'd been trying so hard to hide from Ryder. She shook her head for a long time and admitted low, "It would've been different if we could register to the Boarlanders. It would've taken the sting off this, but we're listed as rogue."

Mason pulled the paperwork from her hands and rifled through to page three as Ryder clung like a barnacle to his forehead. "I'm not a rogue, and neither are you. Neither is Ryder." Mason jammed his finger at the box on his paperwork that said *Mate*. He'd written her name in bold, dark capital letters. *Rebecca Anderson*. "It sucks we had to register, but even if we can't marry, or claim each other legally yet, we're bound right here on this legal document."

Stunned, Beck took the stack from him and stared at her name written proudly in the box. Fumbling, she rifled through her paperwork and held up page three. Mason looked up from where she'd printed his name neatly, and a slow smile transformed his face. "So, I was thinking. Today wasn't our choice, and it was a forced, raw deal, sure. But it's also kind of important for you and me and Ryder, so I planned something."

"Planned what?" Ryder asked in that cute little voice of his.

Mason pulled him from his shoulders and settled Ryder on his feet next to Beck. "I planned a surprise adventure, but we have to go back home to do it. And it means we can't be fiddlefuckin' around town too long because we need daylight."

Ryder formed his mouth into a *F* shape, but Mason said, "Don't say fiddlefuckin'. That's an adult word."

Ryder clacked his mouth closed. Then excitedly, he said, "I never been on a surprise adventure before." He bounced beside Beck, clutching her power pants in his little fists.

Home. Mason had said they had to go

home, and it was the first time he had said that to her. Beck bit her lip hard so she wouldn't lose it in front of the boys.

Pulling his hand, she led Mason toward a fountain in a park next to the courthouse, and then she gave Ryder a few coins to make wishes with.

"Tell me what's going on in your head," Mason said as he sat on the stone ledge of the water feature. He pulled her between his knees and cocked his head, his eyes lightening just a shade. "Don't think, just tell me. What was that look for?"

"I've been working so hard to get Ryder out of that little apartment in Douglas. I mean, my focus has been on building a better life, and this whole time, I thought a better life meant more money, a bigger place to live, a puppy, better clothes. Those were the thoughts that kept pushing me to go for bigger jobs while Robbie was falling farther behind on his child support payments. I was determined to give Ryder this cushy life and prove that I could make up for Robbie's shortcomings."

"I wish for a puppy!" Ryder yelled and threw a penny over his shoulder.

Mason tossed him a quick look and then

lowered his voice. "And now you're settling for an old trailer park."

God, she would've laughed if he didn't look so concerned. "Not settling, Mason. I see things differently now. In Damon's mountains, Ryder will grow up with other kids like him. Dragons, ravens, falcons, and bears. He won't have to feel alone like I did growing up. You know what Brooke asked me the last time I was visiting the Ashe Crew?"

"What?"

"She was wondering if you would be interested in helping Tagan coach a baseball league for the kids in the mountains. And not just shifter kids, but creating teams with the locals who are too far out to travel to Saratoga for baseball season. Humans and shifters, and Ryder could play ball without having to hide his strength or agility. I could imagine you coaching him, and him being a part of something. Mason—" Beck's voice cracked, so she tried again. "I don't care about the money, or living in an old trailer, or any of that. I care about the smile on Ryder's face. Even when his lips aren't smiling, his eyes are. So yeah. Maybe I'm settling for something different than I imagined, but only because it's better than I could imagine."

Mason dragged her against his chest and sipped at her lips. "You know I'll coach his team, right?"

She huffed a laugh and rested her forehead against his. "Somehow, yeah, I knew that you would be interested."

"Tagan's going down. Ashe Crew versus Boarlander and Gray Back kids."

"Gonna get a C-Team trophy," she murmured through a giggle.

"C-Team," he repeated softly.

"I thought Ryder wouldn't ever have opportunities like that. And rumor has it Aviana is going to start teaching a school for the shifter kids right outside of Damon's boundary next year, so the human kids in the area can attend, too. If we stay here, he'll have a foot in both worlds, Mason. I know my job will end, likely after the vote, whether we're given our rights back or not. But every time I think of leaving the trailer park and going back to my old life, I get this sick feeling in the pit of my stomach. I imagine seeing Robbie around town with his new family and having to explain to Ryder why he won't acknowledge him. I imagine how much it'll hurt both of us being away from you, and my mind revolts against the idea of not fighting for a life here.

With you."

Mason brushed his fingertip down her cheek. He was quiet for a long time, just drinking her in, but finally, he reached in his pocket and pulled out a knife. It was small and finely crafted with a polished wooden handle and a closed blade. On the handle the letters *MC + RA* were carved neatly. "My people don't bite to claim," he murmured low, looking around. "We use a ceremonial knife. Two slices to represent our tusks, right under your collarbone. It's against my peoples' laws to mark anyone other than another boar." Mason flicked open the blade, and it shone in the sun. "It's against human laws for me to mark you."

"Mason," she whispered, hope blooming in her chest as he unbuttoned her jacket.

"I had Beaston make me this knife just for this. For you. I don't care what anyone else tells me I can and can't do. You're mine, and I'm yours." He jerked his head at Ryder, who was squatted down, watching a line of ants on the stone walkway. "That boy is mine." Mason pushed her jacket off her left shoulder and moved the thin strap of her top to the side. "I didn't plan on doing it like this, but I haven't seen Esmerelda in a week. You wrote my name on that paperwork, you're telling me you're staying here, and it feels right to do this now. This is our moment, Beck. I'm taking this day back for us. Fuck anyone telling us we can't be bound." Mason blinked slow and raised his blazing blue eyes from her collar bone to her face. "Do you want my mark, Beck? Do you want all of me?"

Beck lifted her chin as her chest heaved. She blew out a steadying breath and nodded. "I've wanted all of you from the moment I saw you."

Mason looked around again, glanced at Ryder, then quick as a snakebite, he cut two long, deep marks beneath her collar bone. The air smelled of pennies, and warmth trickled down her chest from the burning cuts, but she couldn't see anything through her tears. Dropping her head with a sob, she melted into his arms and dampened his shirt with her happiness.

Gently, Mason cupped the back of her head and rocked them from side-to-side. "Someday, I'm going to put my last name on you, and someday I'll fill out paperwork that binds me to Ryder as well. I swear I will. Everything will be okay, Beck. I promise. We aren't there yet, but we will be. But for now, this is what I can offer you. An old trailer park, some crazy-ass friends, and all of me."

"Mason?" Ryder asked softly, his eyes big and yellow in the sunlight where he stood right beside them. "Is Mommy okay?"

Mason swallowed hard and reached out for Ryder. "Yeah, boy. We're all okay." He drew him in beside Beck, and she wrapped her arms around her boys and quieted her weeping. She'd thought today would be the worst day of her life, but she'd been wrong. Mason had dug deep and grabbed ahold of the bright side, then offered it to her on his open palm.

She was claimed.

Claimed.

No one had ever picked her, but Mason had just said *fuck everyone's rules* and marked her for himself despite the tornado swirling all around them.

He's chosen her, chosen Ryder, chosen to fight for them.

She reveled in the sting of the marks on her chest because the pain meant they were deep and would scar. And damn, she wanted them to scar noticeably. She would wear tank tops and show everyone that Mason, the protective, sweet, quiet, strong boar shifter had picked *her*.

Today was supposed to be the worst, but

instead, the man she loved had just turned it into a day that would rival all other good days.

TWENTY-ONE

"But what if I cain't swim?" Ryder asked as Mason slathered his wiry little arms in sunscreen.

"I got you a life jacket, and you'll be in a tube with me and your mom. We won't let you sink."

"I like your swim trunks," Bash said to Ryder as he walked by with Big Blue, the cooler Mason had filled with beer and juice boxes. "And your yellow eyes!"

Mason frowned at Ryder and said, "Little buddy, your eyes are pretty yellow. Are you just excited, or do you want to Change before we go?"

"I'm okay, Mason. I'm tough."

He wouldn't admit it out loud, but Mason had bought the little blue shark swim trunks for Ryder because they were the same color as his navy ones. Yeah, he wanted to match the kid. The guys would rag him mercilessly if he told them how soft his heart had gone, so he would keep that little tidbit for pillow-talk tonight with Beck. She was always really mushy after they had sex. Maybe she was still a little broken from how Robbie had treated her body, or maybe she just had a tender heart. Either way, Mason loved every freaking thing about her.

Ryder arched his gaze to Clinton as he walked by. And to Mason's utter disbelief, Clinton ruffled Ryder's hair gently until the little boy giggled and play punched at his leg. Clinton ducked and wove, fists up in the air and an easy grin on his face. What the crap was going on? Hell froze over or something. Clinton didn't do easy, normal moments.

The shadow boxing bear shifter scowled at Mason and asked, "What are you lookin' at?" Then he sauntered off without another look back and yep, there was Crazy Clinton again.

"Hey, did you park your truck at the end of the line?" Mason called.

Clinton flipped him off over his shoulder, which he supposed was a yes. Today, they were floating the river, something Clinton had been begging to do for a month. Well, actually he'd wanted to get sloppy drunk and float the river, but one out of two wasn't bad since they were going to cut him off at beer five. When Ryder had told Mason that his dad was supposed to take him to swim lessons this summer, but had bailed for work instead, he found himself determined to make up for that asshole's shortcomings. He would teach Ryder to swim before the weather turned, but for today, he was going to have some fun with the crew so that Ryder didn't look back on the day Beck was forced to register him and have a bad taste in his mouth. Mason didn't want him to suffer when he looked back on today.

Kirk walked by, his arm slung over Ally's slim shoulders. She wore a green bikini that didn't hide much of the tattoos that covered her back and arm. Good for her. She used to hide her ink because she didn't want to share her story, but over the past couple of months, her modesty and insecurities had slipped away. Probably hanging with a crew of party-lovin', constantly-Changing, semi-nudist shifters helped.

"You coming?" Kirk asked.

"We're waiting on Momma," Ryder said. "Momma!! Hurry up or we're gonna miss the river!"

Mason chuckled and told him, "Don't rush her, boy. We're still waiting on Harrison, Emerson, and Audrey, too. Don't worry. We won't miss the river."

When Mason stood and turned toward his trailer, he was stunned to stillness at the sight of his mate. She was walking this way, her bird-fine frame on display under a purple triangle bikini top and holey cut-off shorts she must've borrowed from one of the girls. They hung loose on her hips in the sexiest way possible. He'd never seen her in anything other than a matching pajama set, matching lingerie, power pants, or crisp, designer jeans under a blouse, but damn, she sure was fitting in now. The black sparkly flip flops on her feet were a little big and clacked with each step she approached, and those long, sexy legs had him adjusting his dick. The afternoon light gleamed off the silver stretch marks over her hips, but it was her cleavage, bouncing enticingly with each step that held his attention for too long. How did he know? Because when he finally managed to rip his gaze away from those perfect tits of hers, she'd shoved her white-rimmed sunglasses up on her head and her gorgeous green eyes were dancing as she offered him that knowing grin he loved so much.

Damn, his woman was beautiful. She pulled her petal-pink towel off her shoulder, exposing the raw, red slices he'd given her a few hours ago. Not just his woman anymore. A slow smile stretched his face. His mate.

Emerson walked beside Beck, chattering on happily in her green two-piece, the swell of her belly leading the way. And on Beck's other side, Audrey was in her white tiger form, mouth open in a soft pant as she strode gracefully toward them, her giant paws spreading on the soft ground with each step. Her tiger loved the water.

The soft tinkling of Beck's laughter filled the clearing. Beck had said Ryder's smile meant the world to her, but Beck was changing, too. Likely more than she realized. Mason had noticed her smiling more, opening up more, relaxing into the crew. A few weeks ago, he'd been at one of the valleys of his life, and standing here, watching Ryder run to Beck, watching her catch him in her arms and spin him as they both peeled into giggles, he thought he couldn't be any happier. What a turnaround. What a complete one-eighty his life had undergone in such a short amount of time.

Gentle movement across the trailer park in the woods beyond captured his attention. There was something in the tree branches. Something blurry, hard to make out, tinged in blue. Mason took a step forward and squinted. As Esmerelda came into focus, his blood chilled to ice, and a horrified sound scratched up his throat. She was hanging from a rope, her body transparent so that he could make out the pine needles behind her. Her neck was broken against the rope, her bare feet swaying gently in the breeze, her white sundress pristine and lifting at the hem, just like he remembered. Almost. Her eyes were open, staring at him, beseeching him as her lips formed the words, *they're coming*.

With a gasp, he closed his eyes. His lungs hardened to rock, like he was the one dangling from that hanging rope.

Mason.

Don't say my name, Essie. Please don't say my name.

"Mason!"

He shook his head hard as Essie's voice morphed into Beck's. His mate's nails were digging into his bicep as she shook him hard. "Mason, what's wrong?" Her tone was pitched high and scared.

Mason forced himself to look back at the trees, but Essie was gone. Just...gone, like she'd never been there at all. He wanted to believe he'd just imagined it, but the chills on his arms wouldn't go away. He rubbed the cold skin on the back of his neck and dragged his horrified gaze back to Beck. She was real. She was real, touchable, and here, and she would never leave him like Essie had.

"I'm okay," he rasped out in a voice he didn't recognize. "We're okay."

Beck looked behind her at where Esmerelda had been hanging, but she shook her head like she didn't see anything. Thank God.

Mason swallowed bile and hugged her tight against his chest so he could hide how much seeing Essie hang from that damned rope was affecting him. She hadn't left him alone like he'd thought, but Beck didn't deserve this. She didn't deserve the taint of Esmerelda's ghost on her big day. Not on the day he'd marked her.

Beck was saying something. Asking a question. Forcing himself to listen, he answered her. "No, it's nothing. I thought I saw something, but I didn't."

Beck's blazing yellow eyes and the frown

that marred her delicate ruddy eyebrows said he wasn't lying well enough, but that couldn't be helped. This was the best he could do after that shock. *They're coming.* He fuckin' knew! He had them! He had Beck claimed, Ryder was his boy no matter genetics or paperwork, so why was Essie still here screwing with him?

After a week of silence, he'd thought the ghost of his past had found rest, but still, Mason was failing her in some way he couldn't understand.

****

Mason's heart was drumming too fast under her face, and Beck took a second look in the direction he'd been staring. His expression had terrified her. It had been as if his heart was being ripped from his body. There was only one thing that could've caused that kind of horror in his eyes, but he'd just lied to her. He was trying to protect her from his past.

Beck hugged his waist tight. "I'm here. You're here, too."

"Yeah," he murmured, but his voice cracked on the word, and his hands rubbed in jerking motions against her back.

Suddenly desperate to get him away from whatever he'd seen, she said, "Come on," and tugged his hand toward the trail that led through the Boarlander woods to Bear Trap Falls.

Up ahead, Ryder was standing with his arms out in a circle at his side, grinning as Audrey sauntered straight toward him, putting her giant face into the circle he'd created. Her purr was so loud that it drowned out the birds in the canopy. This was their game. Ryder liked to pretend he was a ringleader in a circus, and Audrey seemed fine playing along.

"Ryder, don't ride Audrey," Beck scolded him.

Too late. Ryder had already grabbed the scruff of her neck and scrambled on her back. "She likes it!"

If he was hurting Audrey, the giant tiger didn't show it. Audrey twitched her tail and smoothed out her gait as Ryder hung on like a tiny tiger jockey. Emerson giggled and snapped a picture of them, and up ahead on the trail, Harrison wore the biggest grin. The alpha watched them with a tenderness that told Beck they wouldn't wait too long to try for cubs of their own.

"I call next!" Bash said through the trees.

"No," Harrison said.

"Why not?" Bash asked, a frown furrowing his dark eyebrows.

"Because you're two-hundred-fifty pounds of grown-ass man, Bash. She ain't a pony, and this ain't your party."

Bash crossed his arms over his chest and muttered, "Fine."

"Whose party is it?" Ryder asked before he stuck his tongue back out and his focus-face returned.

"It's yours," Mason said.

Beck sighed a breath of relief that he seemed to be thawing out again.

"Because we had to tell 'Merica that I'm an owl-boy?"

"Yeah, and because me and your mom are bound now. And look here."

Ryder slid off Audrey's back like a nimble little monkey and squinted at Beck's shoulder where Mason was pointing.

"You got two boo-boos, Momma."

Bash snickered. "Well, it would be weird if she had three boobies!"

Ryder grabbed his stomach and doubled over laughing. "Not boobies!"

"Is that what I think it is?" Emerson asked, running her finger just under the marks.

Heat flashed up from Beck's chest to her cheeks and settled there. With an emotional smile, she nodded. "Mason gave it to me right after we registered, right there beside the courthouse."

"Oh, my gosh!" Emerson exclaimed, pulling her into a gentle embrace.

Bash came charging through the woods like a rhino and lifted her and Mason up in a back-cracking bear hug.

Mason was laughing now, Esmerelda apparently forgotten, and he ruffled Bash's black hair. "Okay, Bash Bear. Don't squeeze my mate too hard. She's got those fine bones, not like a big old bear."

"I knew she was gonna be one of us," Bash said too loud as he set them down too hard. "Emerson, didn't I say that? I said day one, publicist is gonna stay here. She had to. She was stayin' in ten-ten. Ten-ten wins again!" Bash whooped loud enough to echo through Boarlander woods and grinned big at each of them.

"Do you need to run?" Harrison asked.

"I need to run!" Bash yelled, right before he spun around and bolted for the river.

"Can I run, too?" Ryder cried.

Cracking up, Beck nodded. "Don't go in the water yet, though," she called as her son blasted off on those fast little legs of his, swim trunks billowing behind him and giving him a little bubble butt.

Mason frowned and yelled, "Bash, don't let him in the water!"

"I'll keep him safe!" Bash called from a distance.

Beck nudged his rock-hard shoulder. "Protective."

"Yeah, about that. My instincts are insane lately. I don't want you or him out of my sight. Is that normal?"

Beck stooped to pick a thorn from the bottom of her flip flop while resting her hand on Mason's forearm for balance. "It's completely normal for me, so probably." Robbie sure didn't have any paternal instincts, but Mason was the sun, and her ex was the darkest night. The two couldn't be compared.

Mason picked her up so fast she left her stomach on the forest floor. He nuzzled his sexy facial scruff against her tender belly until she was squirming and shouting laughter. His biceps bulged as he rested her over his shoulder and strode through the woods with a strong, confident gait behind the other Boarlanders.

"Just to warn you, I'm gonna be starin' at those sexy tits of yours all day, so keep your little smirks to yourself."

"No deal. When did you have time to plan a floating trip?"

"When you and Ryder were down in Saratoga the other day for that Lumberjack Wars meeting with Parks and Rec. I went and got the tubes from Moosey's Bait and Barbecue, the bait side. They had a little lifejacket, too, that looked the right size for Ryder. I even got a tube for Big Blue." Mason set her down and pointed to where Kirk was shoving the cooler into a square floaty.

Bash had placed himself between Ryder and the river waves lapping at the beach. "I bought girl drinks, too, and rainbow umbrellas so you can feel fancy."

Ally lifted a bright red fruity beer from the cooler and handed it to Beck while Mason went to work helping Kirk and Clinton duct tape a bunch of giant yellow inner tubes together. Across the river, a commotion snatched Beck's attention.

"Yooohooo," called a petite, red-head with thick glasses, a floppy straw hat, and a yellow polka-dotted saggy tankini. The Gray Backs filed out of the woods behind her.

"Hey, Willa!" Emerson yelled with a wave.

"Hell, yeah," Kirk said. "Now it's a C-Team party."

"The Ashe Crew is meeting us down river." Creed, the dark-haired alpha of the Gray Backs called through cupped hands, "Hey, Ryderman!"

"Hi Mister Creed!"

"Congratulations on owning your owl today, buddy!"

"Hooo, hooo!" Ryder called.

Her son was practically vibrating with pride as Beck snapped him into his life jacket, and a well of excitement bubbled up her throat. Today had turned out so differently than she'd thought it would.

They piled into their inner tubes, Ryder into the smallest one, and rowed clumsily with cupped, splashing hands to the middle of the river toward the Gray Backs, who were doing an equally horrid job of steering. They were all cracking up by the time they reached each other and linked up. And behind them, Kirk, Bash, and Clinton jumped all the way over the falls and into the river with huge cannon-ball splashes. Ryder got so excited, he squeezed his juice box all over himself and giggled uncontrollably when the rowdy Boarlanders popped out of the water right beside his tube and splashed him. A slow-floating quarter-mile down river, and the Ashe Crew was waiting in the shallows, true to their word, and with a couple of kiddos around Ryder's age. Wyatt was the blue-eyed bear shifter son of the Ashe Crew alpha, Tagan, and his mate, Brooke. And Bruiser and Diem's daughter, Harper, linked up her little tube to the boys' too. She was a striking girl, with dark hair and one soft brown eye like Diem's, the other blue with an elongated reptilian pupil. But despite the fire-breathing dragon that resided inside of her, she was polite and gentle with Ryder when they splashed around.

When Mason swam up behind Beck and rested his elbows on her tube, then leaned in and nuzzled her neck, another layer of happiness washed over her. Looking around at the different crews who were greeting each other like they hadn't seen each other in months instead of days, and under Mason's easy affection with the soundtrack of Ryder's laughter echoing through the river valley, this incredible sense of belonging drifted over her like a warm, comfortable blanket.

And now she had another reason to fight for the shifter rights vote.

Because someday, someway, she and Ryder and Mason were going to register and pledge as official Boarlanders.

TWENTY-TWO

Mason readjusted Ryder's weight in his lap so he could drape his arm around Beck's shoulders. A distracted smile still lingered on her lips as she swayed from side to side with the rocking motion of Clinton's truck. She was happy. Mason could sense it coming off her in waves, and damn, what it did to his animal. Hoof stomping, chest up, head held high, his animal hadn't ever been a prideful creature, but today he was.

On the other side of the truck bed, Kirk was rubbing his mate Ally's shoulder absently as she dozed off. Usually, Clinton drove like a bat out of hell, but today, he'd acted almost normal. Maybe 1010 was working its magic on him, too.

The sun was setting behind the mountains, painting the sky in neon pinks and oranges, casting Beck's face in a pretty glow. She smiled up at him, as if she could hear his thoughts. Hell, maybe she could. He'd never marked a woman before. It had been against the rules of the boar people to give Essie one because she was human, and he'd cared deeply about what his people thought about him back then. Now, all he cared about was Beck, Ryder, and the inhabitants of Damon's mountains.

Clinton pulled under the Boarland Mobile Park sign and onto the new gravel road. He parked in his yard over the scorched words he'd burned into his weeds and, exhausted from the day, they all climbed out of the truck. Ryder was still hanging on, but Mason would bet his tusks he would sleep like a winter grizzly tonight.

But when he turned for 1010, there was a familiar, beat-up old white Ford truck parked on the new concrete pad beside it. And on the front porch rocking chairs, Beaston and Aviana sat with matching smiles.

"Beaston!" Kirk called with a wave. The others greeted him, too, but the feral-eyed bear shifter only nodded a greeting, his glowing green eyes never straying from Ryder.

With a frown, Mason led Ryder and Beck to the porch. The boy hadn't met the Novaks yet, but not for lack of Mason trying. It seemed Beaston had trouble being separated from his raven boy more than a few yards, and he'd grown protective and unwilling to take him out of the trailer he shared with Aviana behind the Grayland Mobile Park.

Beaston was cupping something gently on his lap and didn't stand as they approached like his dark-haired mate, Aviana, did. Instead, he cocked his head at Ryder and murmured, "I'm Beaston."

Ryder had gone quiet, and Mason understood. Beaston's eyes glowed like a demon's, and the air around him was heavy with dominance.

"Tell him hi," Beck encouraged him.

"Hi," Ryder said shyly, his eyes on the floorboards.

"Introduce yourself," Beck murmured, inching him forward by the shoulders.

"My name's Ryder Layton Anderson and I'm five years old and I live in a trailer park."

Beaston cracked a crooked smile, just for an instant before his eyes went curious again. "I came here to see you."

"Why?" Ryder asked in that little squeaky voice of his.

"I have something to show you."

"Is it a puppy?"

"No, but it's the most important thing to me. The best thing." He held out his cupped hands, and on his palms sat a tiny, fluffy, jet-black chick with a glossy, black beak and big round eyes that blinked curiously at Ryder. "This is my raven boy, Weston. Someday, you'll call him Wes."

Ryder's eyes went round, and Mason knelt beside him to get a better look at Beaston's son. "He's already shifted?"

"Early," Beaston said with a nod. "I wanted to come today. Wanted to come to the river for Ryder, but Weston Changed and..."

Aviana settled her hand on her mate's tensed shoulder and whispered, "It's okay."

"I had a dream," Beaston said, his eyes steady on Ryder. "A black raven and a snow white owl were flying over a crowd. Everything was loud. Cheering. They flew as one. Happy. My Aviana will only bear me cubs now, and Weston will be my only raven boy, and you...you will be like his brother. You'll be fierce. Strong." Beaston's eyes blazed like green flames as his voice dipped lower. "And do you know what they will call you?"

"What?" Ryder whispered.

"They will call you Air-Ryder, Son of the

Beast Boar, Blood Brother to the Novak Raven."

Chills blasted up Mason's arms, and he jerked his eyes to Beck, who looked equally as stunned.

"Who," Mason asked, fully aware that Beaston's dreams had never been wrong. He had the sight, like his mother before him. "Who will call him that?"

Beaston lifted those wild green eyes to Mason as a sly grin spread across his face. "Everyone."

TWENTY-THREE

Mason stood leaned against Ryder's open doorframe, arms crossed over his chest as he watched him sleep. The little boy's lips were parted, and his face was completely relaxed. He used to think boar offspring were the cutest, but now that seemed ridiculous. Ryder was the cutest. Little fluffy owlet, always wanting Mason or Beck to hold him when he Changed. Mason had tucked one of his downy gray and white feathers into an empty matchbox for safekeeping since Ryder wouldn't be this little forever.

Beaston's dream proved that. Someday he would grow up, and Mason wouldn't get to cuddle the little owl anymore. He would get manly hugs and back slaps. *Son of the Beast Boar*. Mason gritted his teeth against the urge to fall apart. He sure didn't feel like The

Barrow anymore.

Beck was in the living room folding laundry and watching some reality show she roped him into sitting through after Ryder went to bed at night. Any other woman, he would've fought it, but Beck liked snuggling and talking about the characters, and damn, he would watch a documentary about water boiling if it made her happy.

She'd been on the warpath since they'd been forced to register. Her days were filled with balancing motherhood and being a champion for the shifters. She had meetings and conference calls, organized events, and bullied the crews into community service with a relentless tenacity. Cora Keller had called Harrison and told him to keep her happy because the work Beck was doing for shifter public relationships was making a huge difference. Even Cora was back to joking on her phone calls, where for a while, she'd been so stressed, like the weight of their future was on her shoulders.

Mason was so fucking proud of Beck for stepping up. She had everyone doing a job, visiting the websites, answering questions, doing community outreach, and volunteering at Parks and Rec events down in Saratoga. At her direction, the girls of the Ashe Crew had built a huge rapport with the surrounding areas at the flea market where they sold their shabby chic furniture and décor. Willa's Worms were now a staple at every bait shop from here to Kansas, and every one of the crews spent more time in town and signed autographs whenever anyone asked.

Beck had her hand in so many pots, and she was the epitome of grace under fire. None of the negativity seemed to get to her. She brushed off the protesters in Saratoga like they were no more than annoying gnats, and yesterday, at a meeting at City Hall, she'd been called out for the first time for her animal. Her cheeks had flushed for a moment, but then she'd lifted her chin proudly in the air and told them, "Damn straight, I'm a snowy owl shifter. I'm proud of where I come from."

She'd stared down that committee, eyes bright yellow and daring them to look away, like some warrior woman ready for battle. Mason had sat there beside her, completely stunned that he'd landed a tough-as-nails woman like her. Just the memory of the fierceness on her face drew up Mason's boar.

Mason tucked the covers around Ryder's little body, wrapping him up like a burrito before he strode into the living room. They'd moved out of 1010 and into his trailer the day after floating the river, and over the last week, Beck and Ryder had fit in easily here. And now, he could barely remember this place without them. They'd stamped their presence here so completely that every room, wall, and floorboard now held a memory of his little family.

Bash had once said Emerson was his air, and Mason hadn't understood the sentiment at the time. But now he did. Beck and Ryder were the oxygen that made him breathe easy and feel normal.

"Let me do the rest," he murmured, gesturing to the laundry basket. Ryder only had what he'd packed for Robbie's, and since the boy loved playing in the dirt, he and Beck were doing laundry constantly now. They soon would need to go back to Douglas and pick up her car and move her out here officially. She hadn't been keen on going back to a place where she'd been cut so deeply, and he understood that.

He could never go back to his first home either.

But looking at Beck now as she smiled up at him from the couch, he didn't have the urge to anymore. Home was where she and Ryder were. Home was here, with the Boarlanders.

Boar-lander. He should've known he was destined for this crew.

Beck opened her mouth to say something, but her attention landed somewhere behind him, and her face transformed into one of horror. Her eyes turned from green to yellow in an instant.

Mason's skin prickled with the cool breeze of wrongness against the back of his neck. He didn't want to turn around, didn't want to see her, but Esmerelda was here, and he couldn't make Beck witness her alone.

Slowly, Mason turned. Essie stood there in the kitchen, eyes so sad, a rope burn deep in her neck. She was tinted blue, transparent, and her hair and white dress fluttered around her in a stiff wind that didn't touch him.

"They're coming." Her lips moved just after the words reached his ears.

"Essie, I moved on, just like you wanted. You have to let me go. You can't come here anymore."

Her eyebrows arched high, and a strangled sound screeched from her throat, as if she wanted to say more but hadn't the power. Her hair whipped about, and the front door ripped open, slammed against the wall with a crash.

And Esmerelda was gone.

Outside, she whispered it again. "They're coming."

She was luring him. He knew it but was powerless to stop his legs from carrying him toward the door.

"Mason," Beck said in a shaking voice. She pulled his hand but, helplessly, he dragged her with him. What was happening to him? He stared down at his legs in horror, willing them to stop.

"Mason, don't go out there!" Beck yelled, her bare feet stuttering against the laminate flooring as she struggled to stop him.

The second his boot echoed onto the porch in the evening light, Beck's hand slipped from his. She stood frozen in the doorway, hair tumbling down her shoulders, eyes round, chest heaving.

Eyes wide with terror, Beck whispered, "I can't move."

Enraged that Essie's power was affecting Beck, Mason looked to the woods and yelled, "I'm here! What do you want from me?"

They're coming. Coming, coming. They're coming. The hissed whispers filled his head, each word cluttering the next. *Coming, coming.*

They're coming.

Mason squatted down and covered his ears. He hated her voice, hated that she was still here haunting him. Hated her. "Gaaah!" he screamed as the volume of her whispers drowned out everything and filled his head.

The noise dipped to nothing so suddenly that Mason opened his eyes, and there she was, right in front of his face. Tears streaming down her translucent cheeks, she said, "Mason, they're here." Esmerelda was blasted backward and disappeared in a puff of cerulean smoke.

The ground rattled under his feet like an earthquake.

"Mason," Clinton said, warning in his voice. He stood on top of his trailer next door, eyes on the woods where trees were shaking. Something awful was coming closer and closer. Shit.

Boom! A gunshot echoed through the valley, and in an instant, Kirk threw his trailer door open. "Ally!" he yelled. His massive silverback ripped out of him, and he charged the woods. Clinton landed hard from where he jumped off his trailer.

"Call the dragon," Mason barked out, but Clinton was already dialing on his cell phone.

"What's happening?" Beck asked in a voice that trembled with terror.

The trailer rattled as the vibration grew closer, and Mason held onto the banister to steady himself. "Beck, stay inside. No matter what you hear, you go in Ryder's closet, and you don't come out. You protect our boy."

Everything was so clear now. So bright. So obvious. He'd been wrong about what Esmerelda had been doing here. She hadn't been telling him to let her go. She'd been warning him against the people who had cut her heart wide open when she'd been alive. She'd been warning him, not because she couldn't let go, but because she wanted him to protect what he'd found—Beck and Ryder. The Boarlanders. He ran for the woods, peeling off his shirt as he went.

"Mason," Beck shrieked. "Is it IESA?"

"No!" He called back at her. He gritted his teeth against the hatred that welled up inside of his chest. "It's the boars."

Emerson ran by as Bash and Harrison melted into the woods in front of him, a deep snarl in their throats. She bolted for Mason's trailer with a gun in her hand. "I'll take care of them!" she called out. Her eyes were full of terror, but her voice was steady, determined.

Good Emerson. Brave human, knowing just what to do so he could focus on the blood he was about to let. Fuckin' Robbie for outing him, and fuckin' Jamison for not being able to let Mason go.

A sick feeling twisted his gut as his boar roared to be set free. Now, he had everything to lose.

Another gunshot boomed through the valley, and the drum of a silverback beating his chest echoed through Boarlander woods. His people were going to war, and their pain would be on him. Their blood would be on his hands.

He could smell them now as he wove through the trees. The thick, dizzying, musty scent of dominant boars tainted the air and filled his senses. The deep-throated squeal of a battle cry blasted through the forest. There would be no talking them down. They weren't here to negotiate his return. They were here to steal everything he loved.

His body broke, bones snapping, muscles stretching, bottom canines elongating into thick, sharp tusks as his body exploded into something monstrous. He hit the ground running on sure-footed hooves. He was fast in this form. Faster than a lightning strike as the trees blurred past him. Harrison and the others had cut them off in the firefly meadow. The raw violence of the bears, the tiger, the silverback, and all the boars pushed fury through his chest. There were too many.

Jamison's giant red boar stood off to the side, eyes blazing the blue of his people. Mason wanted to gut him. Wanted to run his tusks through his belly and watch him die in his own entrails for trespassing in his mountains. Bash was in trouble, though, under a pile of four razorbacks. None of the boars could touch Mason or Jamison's size, but frenzied by bloodlust, they had the numbers and single-minded killing instincts that made them bold and relentless. Mason shifted his stride and hit the back of a boar head on, gouging his thick hide with his long tusks.

He shook his powerful neck, stabbing, battling, protecting Bash's weak side—his back. The air smelled like iron, and the boars grew in number, as if Jamison had called another wave. He lost his mind. Lost his thoughts other than *kill*. Other than *defend them*. Other than *save them*.

Flashes like photographs punctuated brief moments between battling. Kirk slamming a white boar against a tree trunk. Harrison's massive grizzly clamping over the thick neck of another. Bash's claws...too close. Audrey's white tiger leaping onto a boar slashing at Harrison's back, her canines open and ready, her claws out, her eyes full of fury. Ally, legs splayed over her four-wheeler, tattoos black against her pale skin, lips pulled back in a battle scream, she popped round after round at the boars that surrounded her.

Pain ripped up his back leg, and Mason went down hard, skidding in the dirt. The second he hit earth, Jamison charged him, the coward. He'd watched from the side until Mason was tired. Until he was down and wounded.

Adrenaline surged through his body, and he struggled to his feet, catching Jamison's full force. The brawler boar had broken off one of his tusks since Mason had last seen him, but his brother was skilled at protecting his weak side, slashing the other like a long blade. Jamison wanted war? He could have his mother fucking war. Mason wasn't the same broken shifter he was when he'd challenged Jamison before. He wasn't depleted and weak. In his time away from his people, he'd spent his efforts logging, putting on muscle, and battling for these mountains beside Damon and the other crews. He wasn't wishing for death anymore. Now, he had so much to survive for. So much to defend.

Jamison hit him like a wrecking ball, but Mason was ready. His legs braced, he skidded through the dirt, locked his tusks with Jamison's and jerked his neck, throwing his brother off balance. Stupid fucker had been brawling with lesser boars, but Mason was a dominant Croy like him. He was a rip-roaring war machine.

Searing pain flashed up the nerve endings in his side as other boars joined Jamison. Assholes didn't know how to fight with honor. They didn't care if it took a hundred of them to kill one, so long as they won. So much ache, so much warmth, but Mason couldn't unlock with Jamison, or his brother would have him gutted in an instant, just like the first time.

Something white blurred by, and the shriek of a pig sounded from behind him. The weight on Mason's body lessened, and in an instant, another white streak dove and lifted. Beck. She was going for their faces, keeping the others off his back. Distracting them.

Clinton's blond bear roared an oath of death and slapped another boar off the pile, then clamped his massive jaws on another.

Crazy Clinton was buying him time.

A battle cry sounded as a set of long, curved, black talons raked across Jamison's left eye. With a grunt of pain, Jamison stumbled, and Mason used his body weight to charge him against a tree.

A hurricane wind broke the trees around the clearing as something massive flew overhead, shadowing the meadow in the promise of flames. Damon.

Beck needed to get out of here because he was about to rain fire. Mason opened his mouth to roar, but Beck wasn't watching him. She was engaged, clawing at Jamison's face as he ran away, shaking his head, trying desperately to dislodge her. But she didn't see what he did. She didn't see the charging boar with his burning eyes on her. One blow full-stop, and she would be ground to dust. No!

Bullets were whizzing by him, so close he could feel the draft. "Mason!" Ally screamed.

I see her. Mason bunched his muscles and bolted for the spotted boar bearing down on his Beck. She was focused on holding onto Jamison's face as he shook his neck and hit a tree, trying to dislodge her. The charging boar was so fast Mason wasn't going to make it on time. *Beck!* He pushed his legs harder, faster, desperate to reach her. The sound of a gunshot connecting with the charging boar echoed, and the animal stumbled. It still wasn't enough—he was already on top of her. Mason hit him hard on the back end, spinning him, but the boar slammed into Beck with the side of his face.

Time slowed to a crawl. His mate spread her snow white wings wide on the impact. Blasting backward in slow motion, she locked her round yellow eyes on Mason and said a million things with a look. *I couldn't keep away. I couldn't leave you to fight alone. I'm sorry.* A tiny dot of red spread onto her white chest feathers, and she opened her beak wide and screamed out a fierce noise.

Behind Beck, the Boarlander woods were alive with roaring, battling bears, and fire. Tagan, Creed, Willa, Beaston, Jason, Matt, Bruiser, Kellen…even Everly's snow-white grizzly shredded boars beside her mate, Brighton. Skyler's falcon dive-bombed into the fight, talons outstretched. They were pure power and fury, but his entire life flickered as Beck twisted around and landed hard in the dirt, skidding several feet before she came to a stop.

Mason ran for her, but was barreled into

by a boar with fur as black as his.

His ears rang with the sound of the boar war, and as he spun sideways from the force of his attacker, Ally's voice came over the blaring sirens in his ears. "I've got her," she yelled, running for Beck's limp body. Kirk was behind her, covering his mate as she risked herself to protect Beck. Was it too late? Was she already gone?

Panic seized Mason. He ran his tusks up the black boar's neck, and he was down, giving Mason time to search frantically for Jamison. His brother stood off to the side, shaking his head and squealing in pain. Beck had ruined the left side of his face. Mason could stop this if only he could reach Jamison. If he could end him, cut off the life of the alpha, the boar-people would stop the attack. Why? Because then Mason would lead them. By boar law, they wouldn't be allowed to attack him anymore. It was why Jamison was here. Mason's existence would always threaten his position with his people. Mason was the only one who could rival him.

Rip, slash, pain, charge, repeat until he was full of fury and bloodlust. Until he was full of hatred for his brother. Jamison had come here to take his life. To take the life of the people he loved. He came knowing this land was protected by Damon. He came knowing he would sacrifice so many of his people to hurt one—his own brother.

Jamison locked eyes on him from the shadows of the tree line. The enormous red boar lifted his head in a challenge, his broken tusk gleaming red in the fading light, blood streaming down the gouge marks that had taken his left eye. Good Beck. Good mate. She'd known just how to stall his brother and buy him time. Beck, Beck, Beck. He would never be okay again if she didn't survive. Jamison's fault. His people had hurt Essie, and now Beck?

Mason dragged a hoof slowly through the dirt and gnashed his teeth. *Fuck you, brother.*

Jamison huffed an enraged roar and charged, and this was it. Mason hadn't ever really escaped his destiny. Hadn't escaped this battle to the death with his brother. Hiding in Damon's mountains hadn't saved him from this moment, when he would accept his fate, whether it brought him victory or death. Mason forced himself to forget about the pain in his body as he pushed off the earth and bolted for Jamison, tusks high and proud. Behind Jamison, a line of boars ran toward

Mason, but Damon's massive blue dragon blew a wall of fire across the clearing, cutting them off. The dragon was giving the Croy boars a fair fight this time around. The glow of the flames reflected off Jamison's coarse red fur and his flexing muscles as he charged, eyes full of hatred.

Mason lowered his head, tusks angled for the monster who had encouraged his people to treat Esmerelda like a pariah and pushed her into that rope. For the monster who had deemed him The Barrow and stripped his pride. For the monster who was trying to take this happy life Mason had eked out. For the monster who brought pain to Damon's mountains. For the monster who had taken Beck from him.

Tonight, he wasn't hiding anymore.

Tonight, he wasn't The Barrow anymore.

He. Was. Beast Boar.

TWENTY-FOUR

Beck forced her eyes open and then winced at the resonating pain that filled her entire body. Someone was talking to her low, begging her to be okay. Ally? She was hugging Beck too tight.

Every bone in Beck's body was broken. They had to be to cause this much pain.

Smoke billowed through the Boarlander woods, but as she shook her head to clear her blurred vision, she saw him. Mason's enormous black boar looked like a monster from legend. His eyes blazed with blue fury as he dragged his black hoof through the dirt, kicking dust over his dark bristled fur. The longer fur along his back was spiked up in agitation, and when he blasted a snort, smoke swirled from his breath. Long cuts decorated his body, pink from how deep into the muscle they'd gone. Along his ribs, she could see the white of his bones. But if he hurt, she couldn't tell. His long tusks had been stained burgundy, and when the red boar across the clearing bolted for Mason, her mate bunched his powerful muscles and charged.

She'd never witnessed such raw power or raw beauty as Mason blasted across the firefly clearing these animals had stolen from them. Mason was violence in motion, a promise of agony, a bringer of destruction. The red boar must be Jamison, Mason's brother. Their shape was the same, much bigger than the other boar-warriors. She would bet her flight feathers he was the Croy who had destroyed Mason's life.

She didn't regret taking his eye.

Her heart pounded against her breastbone as they neared each other. Faster and faster they ran, and when they clashed, a wave of power pulsed from their collision, causing Ally to stagger backward and clutch Beck harder against her chest, hands tight on her wings.

"Oh my gosh," Ally whispered in awe as the boars battled, slicing, ripping, shredding each other mercilessly in a fight that would end in one of their deaths. There was no other way.

Behind them, Damon landed in front of the flames and roared a deafening, prehistoric roar that rattled the earth.

And with one last blurred, flurry of ferocity, it was done.

Mason stood over Jamison's limp body, swaying on his hooves, but victorious. And all around them, chaos reigned as the boars disengaged from their battles and fled. Animals rushed by them with their giant, bloody tusks low as they escaped. Kirk blocked them with his body, shielding Ally and Beck from the panicked boar shifters.

Mason blasted a snort and dragged his feral gaze away from the dead, red boar. How gutted he must've felt in the moment he locked eyes with her. He'd just killed his brother to end the war and save them all.

Beck cried out and tested her wings, but her left one wouldn't work right. She needed to be with him, to touch and reassure him that everything was going to be all right. Someday, everything would be okay again.

"Give her to me," Willa's mate, Matt, said. He pulled a struggling Beck from Ally's arms and pressed her onto the ground, then felt around her wing. He was naked and covered in soot and blood. His bright blue eyes got a faraway look as he pressed around the blindingly painful part of her outstretched wing. "Gray Backs fight all the damned time. We could set bones for a living. This is going to"—*crack*—"hurt."

Beck shrieked in agony. Where was Mason? He wouldn't let her feel pain like this. *Mason!*

She turned her head to the side and forced her eyes open. Smoke and fire billowed behind Mason as he went to his knees with a grunt. *No.* No, no, no. He was going to be okay. He had to be.

But his wounds didn't make sense. She couldn't comprehend how she could see so much injury yet he still looked at her, resolve pooling in his eyes.

"Oh shit," Matt said. "Damon! We need help!" Matt bolted for Mason, skidded on his knees in the dirt next to him as Mason fell to his side. Dust rose around him with the force. Matt was working on him, and then Beaston was there, and Harrison and Bash. As they covered Mason completely from her sight, Clinton appeared through the smog, covered in streaks of ash and long, seeping gashes. He was gripping the back of his hair, and his bright gray eyes were rimmed with moisture. He paced tightly, eyes never leaving Mason.

"Come on, you mother fucker," he screamed. "Live!"

A sick hollowness filled Beck's chest. If she lost him, she would never be okay. It wasn't like with Robbie. Mason was really hers. Hers to love, hers to protect, and she'd failed him. If she'd have been stronger, more thorough raking her talons down Jamison's face, Mason wouldn't be in the dirt now.

Desperate to be with him, she struggled out of Ally's grasp and hopped through the grass.

"Keep her back," Harrison ordered, pointing a blood-soaked finger at her. "She doesn't need to see this."

His eyes were scared. She'd never seen Harrison scared, and Bash was pressing all his weight on his hands, holding together the skin on Mason's ribs. A tear streaked down the soot on Bash's face.

Ally scooped her up before she could reach him, and Beck went mad. Just…insane, trying to escape her hold. She clawed and beat her wings against the woman, shrieking out in fury because Mason was hers. Hers!

And then Damon was there, human,

holding a giant bag of first-aid supplies, and the Ashe Crew and the Gray Backs formed a loose circle. Clinton was screaming curses at Mason, and Harrison's voice was panicked as he gave the others orders.

Beck tried so hard to Change back, but she couldn't. She was stuck and helpless, and Ally was carrying her toward the four-wheeler now. Kirk was blocking the others from her sight with his massive shoulders, and Beck hated everything. A long, mournful cry left her beak, followed by another and another. Her broken wing had been nothing compared to the agony that stabbed at her heart.

For the rest of her life, this moment would be etched into her mind. The sadness in Kirk's eyes as he watched her cry out. The glimpses of the crews trying to save Mason. The fire and the smoke. The way her lungs burned and her chest constricted with the first thoughts of how dark her life would be if she lost her mate.

She stopped fighting Ally. What was the use? Beck was nothing but a weak and broken shell now.

She needed to go to Ryder. If Mason was really gone, the heartache would resonate through her son's life, too.

She needed to hold him and reassure herself she still had purpose because, right now, she felt as if her heart had been plucked from her chest.

Beck closed her eyes against the unending pain in her middle.

She needed Ryder to remind her to breathe.

TWENTY-FIVE

Mason groaned and squinted his eyes at the sunshine blasting a laser beam of light onto his closed eyelid. Something was scratching his stomach. It was a strange sensation, like the tingling he got when his leg fell asleep. His throat was dry, and his body felt like Damon had burned him to crispy bacon. But when he forced his eyes open and looked down at his chest, half hidden by bed sheets, he realized it wasn't fire that had nearly killed him. The boar war came back to him in a flood as he beheld the long, half-healed gashes that covered his torso. Between two scars was a field mouse with giant testicles, walking over his stomach like he was searching Mason for potato chips.

"Hi, Nards," he croaked in a hoarse voice. The mouse looked up at him with those round eyes of his, wiggled his nose and whiskers a few times, and then hopped off him and down the comforter to the floor.

Mason frowned up at the saggy, white ceiling of 1010. Why wasn't he in his own trailer recovering?

"I made them take you here for the magic mojo," Bash said from a chair next to the bed. The titan looked exhausted and was fully bearded. How had he grown so much facial hair so fast? "You been out four days. We been taking turns watching you. Beck won't hardly leave you, but she had to take Ryder out for a while. He was going wild all cooped up." Bash scrubbed his hand down his face, and his usual smiling green eyes looked hollow. He dipped his voice to a ragged whisper. "I thought you left us again."

The raw vulnerability in Bash's admission unfurled a new ache in Mason's chest cavity. "I told you, Bash Bear. I'm not leavin' again." Mason struggled upward and clutched his head when a bout of dizziness took him. When the blanket slipped to his hips, he froze at the sight of his stomach.

"You look like one of them tic-tac-toe boards with a bunch of Xs," Bash said, the hint of a smile returning to his tone.

A moment of insecurity took him when he thought of Beck looking at him like this.

"She's been tracing them while she talks to you." Bash rested his elbows on his knees and clenched his hands. "If you're worried about Beck wantin' to fuck you still, you don't have to. She don't see your scars at all. She just sees you."

Mason swallowed hard and nodded his thanks to Bash. "She's okay then? Is everyone okay?"

"We got new scars decorating our bodies, but yeah. Everyone lived. Your people are fucked up."

Mason let off a long, relieved sigh and closed his eyes against the weight that lifted from his shoulders. "They aren't my people anymore, Bash Bear." He stood on unsteady legs and stumbled into the bathroom. His reflection in the mirror was haunting, but he was still alive. Alive. He'd thought there hadn't been a shot in hell of his survival after he'd fought Jamison. As he'd felt his life slipping away under the frantic attempts of his crew to save him, he'd thought he would never know if Beck lived, or if Ryder would grow up okay. He'd fought to stay awake, desperate to live for them. He owed the people who had worked so hard to put him back together again. And now Bash said Beck was okay, and suddenly, he didn't have to worry about the boar people anymore. He'd hidden for so long, but no more. They wouldn't come after him again. Not without Jamison leading them on his quest for vengeance.

Mason had killed his brother. He winced as he remembered when they'd been young—before Jamison had gone mad with power. They had been close.

He rested on his locked arms against the sink and frowned at himself in the mirror, then to feel human again, he ran water over his hair and face, brushed his teeth, considered a shave but he wanted to see Beck bad. Unsteady on his feet, he shoved his legs into the pair of jeans on the floor. But when he tried to escape the room, he was blocked by a twin mattress that took up the hallway.

"What's this?" Mason asked.

"That's where Clinton slept while you were dead." Bash followed him out of the bedroom and through the kitchen to the living room, where other mattresses were strewn among the green couches.

"Did everyone sleep in ten-ten?" Mason asked, stunned.

"The Boarlanders did, and Damon slept on the floor by your bed at nights, worrying over you somethin' fierce. I never seen the dragon look like that. He'll be wanting me to call him to tell him you're awake. The other crews only visited during the day. Willa brought you that can of worms over there." Bash pointed to a cardboard container on the woodgrain kitchen counter. "She said they were her favorites and named them all Mason."

Mason looked around the trailer and raked his hand through his damp hair. He couldn't believe they'd gone to battle against the boar-people like they had, and now this?

"I need to see Beck," he croaked out. "And Ryder."

"They're off near Bear Trap Falls catchin' frogs."

"I've never seen frogs at the falls."

"Well, your mate ain't been out of this trailer much, so I told her there was. You need to eat somethin'."

"I will," Mason promised as he staggered out of 1010 and down the porch stairs.

Clinton was replanting the rose bushes he'd ripped out of the landscaping but stood slowly when he saw Mason. "Hey, asshole."

Mason huffed a laugh. Clinton cared. He

just didn't know how to show it.

"Hey, asshole," he muttered.

The corner of Clinton's mouth curved up quick before he ripped the newly planted rose bush out of the ground and threw it in the yard. Then he crossed his arms over his chest and arched his blond brows high, daring Mason to rag him.

Mason heaved a sigh and turned for the woods, hiding his private smile. Clinton would always be crazy, and that used to bother him, but not anymore.

As he made his way through Boarlander woods, the sun was so bright that it saturated everything in a vibrant green. Moss and wild grass, pine needles and ferns—it was stunning but almost hurt his sensitive eyes to look at. The ground was soft and rich with the ozone scent that said it had rained while he'd been unconscious.

Long before he set foot on the beach, he heard them—his Beck and Ryder.

They were drawing something in the sand and talking low about how the frogs must be asleep.

Mason hesitated along the edge of the beach, just to take in this moment. He wasn't gone like Esmerelda. He wouldn't haunt them or miss out on their lives. He was here. His body hurt like hell, but feeling pain meant he was alive.

Beck froze, her red-gold curls lifting gently in the wind. Slowly, she stood and turned, her face breathtakingly hopeful. She closed her eyes and sighed with relief, then made her way over the sand to him, her arms out like she couldn't wait to touch him.

She wrapped him up in a tight hug and let off a soft sob. Mason swallowed hard, over and over, to hold onto control over his emotions. Hugging her shoulders tightly, he murmured, "It's over, Beck. We're okay."

"Mason!" Ryder yelled, his face brightening as he blasted toward him on those quick little legs of his.

Mason chuckled as the boy hit him full speed on the leg and wrapped his frail arms around his jeans.

"Hey, Air-Ryder," Mason said, hand on top of the boy's soft hair to convince himself this moment really belonged to him.

Beck sniffled and lifted her bright green eyes to his, a smile on her face. "I thought we lost you."

"Never," he whispered fiercely, brushing a light touch down her neck. God, she looked so beautiful with the sunlight glowing across her cheeks. He couldn't believe she was his. Couldn't believe she'd chosen him.

Beck inhaled deeply and looked down at Ryder. "You remember what we talked about?"

Ryder lifted big round eyes to Mason, and his bottom lip quivered. "I got in trouble from Momma."

"Uh, oh. For what?" Mason asked.

"Show him," Beck murmured.

A frown marring his little face, Ryder took off his T-shirt and pointed to a barely-there scrape on the tip of his shoulder.

"What happened?" Mason said, kneeling to get a better look.

Ryder's eyes rimmed with tears, but he blinked hard, like he was trying to be strong. "Momma told me you made those marks on her chest because she was yours."

"Yeah?"

"Well…I wanted to be yours, too." Ryder's lip poked out farther, and he fell against Mason's chest, hugging his neck tight.

"You made that cut?" Mason asked, shocked.

"Uh huh." Ryder's voice sounded small and ashamed.

Mason blew out a steadying breath and pushed him back to arm's length so he could show him the honesty in his eyes when he made this promise. "Ryder, I won't leave you. You're my boy. You, me, and your mom...we're stuck like glue now, okay?"

Ryder nodded but didn't look convinced, and he got it. Robbie had left Beck so easily. He'd left Ryder, too, and had been cruel when he spent any time with him. He could understand how the boy wanted something that told him Mason wouldn't go back on his word like his real dad. Mason frowned and sighed. "You want a mark that says you're my boy?"

Ryder nodded, his big teary eyes steady on Mason.

"It'll hurt for a minute," he warned him.

"I'm strong like an owl."

Shit, he was going to lose it. Mason blinked hard a couple times, then told him, "You ask your mom if it's okay."

"Can he?" Ryder asked.

When Mason dragged his gaze to Beck's, she was crying and nodding, her arms crossed over her chest like she was trying to keep her heart inside.

Mason took a long, steadying breath, then

pulled the knife Beaston had made him from the back pocket of his jeans. "Look away," he murmured, and when Ryder squeezed his eyes tightly closed, Mason made a quick, inch-long cut deep enough to leave a thin scar, right under his collar bone.

It bled for a few seconds before Ryder's shifter healing kicked in and sealed it up. Mason had a moment of panic at the thought of hurting him, but now Ryder was grinning big, staring at the mark. "Now you cain't leave me." Ryder hugged Mason's neck up tight.

Mason stood slowly, taking Ryder with him in the cradle of his arm. He drew Beck against his side and said, "Now you're both my family."

A light touch rested on his back, and he turned to find Audrey smiling up at him with emotion welling in her eyes. And then Emerson was there, and Ally, hugging the three of them. Harrison gripped his shoulder, Kirk ruffed up his hair, and Bash nearly broke him in half with one of those resounding back claps. Clinton stood leaned against a tree, his chin tucked to his chest, watching them all. He wasn't even scowling.

"It's good to have you back, man," Harrison murmured.

But his alpha didn't see. He'd never even come close to leaving. Not when he'd tried to live away from the Boarlanders, and not when he'd been fighting for his life.

Everything was here.

Mason ran the pad of his thumb across the dampness on Beck's cheek and smiled at the tender-hearted woman who had given him so much. He hugged his little Air-Ryder, Son of the Beast Boar, closer and kissed Beck's lips—just a gentle sip to tell her he loved her.

It didn't matter where he came from or what people had called him in his past life. It didn't matter the assumptions the boar people had made about him. He'd discovered something amazing here in Damon's mountains. He'd stumbled down a long and broken road to end up in a place he could've never imagined.

Here, in this old C-Team trailer park, he was a friend.

He was a mate.

He was a dad.

And from this moment on, he would proudly be known as a Boarlander.

Want More of the Boarlanders?

The Complete Series is Available Now

Other books in this series:

Boarlander Boss Bear
(Boarlander Bears, Book 1)

Boarlander Bash Bear
(Boarlander Bears, Book 2)

Boarlander Silverback
(Boarlander Bears, Book 3)

Boarlander Cursed Boar
(Boarlander Bears, Book 5)

About the Author

T.S. Joyce is devoted to bringing hot shifter romances to readers. Hungry alpha males are her calling card, and the wilder the men, the more she'll make them pour their hearts out. She werebear swears there'll be no swooning heroines in her books. It takes tough-as-nails women to handle her shifters.

Experienced at handling an alpha male of her own, she lives in a tiny town, outside of a tiny city, and devotes her life to writing big stories. Foodie, wolf whisperer, ninja, thief of tiny bottles of awesome smelling hotel shampoo, nap connoisseur, movie fanatic, and zombie slayer, and most of this bio is true.

Bear Shifters? Check
Smoldering Alpha Hotness? Double Check
Sexy Scenes? Fasten up your girdles, ladies and gents, it's gonna to be a wild ride.

For more information on T. S. Joyce's work,
visit her website at
www.tsjoycewrites.wordpress.com

Made in the USA
Thornton, CO
02/23/23 19:25:18

33fa8bad-df56-451c-8b3a-3c9405ec5f6bR01